PRISONERS OF HOPE

IN CHALK CREEK, GEORGIA

a novel by

MARGARET M. LANDHAM

authorHOUSE®

AuthorHouse™
1663 Liberty Drive
Bloomington, IN 47403
www.authorhouse.com
Phone: 1-800-839-8640

First published by AuthorHouse 11/23/2009

ISBN: 978-1-4490-3814-4 (e)
ISBN: 978-1-4490-3816-8 (sc)

Library of Congress Control Number: 2009910812

Printed in the United States of America
Bloomington, Indiana

This book is printed on acid-free paper.

DEDICATION

This story is dedicated to the legion of young, and some not so young, men and women who taught many generations of America's rural youth. In spite of discomforts, discouragements and even dangers, they took "book learning" to the back woods of this nation.

In 1647, the General Court of Massachusetts passed a law stating that every town of fifty householders must hire a schoolmaster. It took the rest of the states many years to follow this lead. In 1931, there were still 149,000 one- room schools in the United States.

The events in this story take place between January and June of 1918. It was inspired by the young teacher who later became my mother.

The personalities included are entirely my own.

ACKNOWLEDGMENTS

For the constructive criticism, information and advice of precious friends and family members I am extremely grateful. Fearing that I might omit someone I shall not use names. You know who you are and how you helped me. Please believe in my sincere appreciation.

There is one however, my sister Sue, who spent tiring hours typing revision after revision after revision of this manuscript. Without her patience, loving and capable help this book would never have happened. And that's the truth.

CONTENTS

Chapter 1--The Leaving

From her upstairs bedroom window the 18-year-old girl looked down at the side yard and the service road that separated it from the pecan orchard.

Friday, January 4, 1918, dawned cold and gray in central Georgia. Thick ground fog lay like a fleecy blanket hovering just beneath the branches of the trees. Up the drive to her right, the cow barns and pasture had completely disappeared under the gray cover. "Surely," she thought, "it will be gone by train time."

She had slept fitfully, trying to forget, to push from her mind the bitterness of last night's confrontation. Like the fog, it permeated her every thought. It was painful to take a deep breath and the tightness in her chest would not go away.

Shivering in her flannel gown, she watched as a dark, square figure walked out of the mist up the narrow road. It was that breathless, fragile moment between darkness and the mauve dawn--that moment when you can barely distinguish objects around you, and artificial light seems a rude intrusion.

The service road led to the barns and the Gypsy Woods, and beyond the woods the train track snaked its way into town. The Gypsy Woods were so called because, for many years, like the arrival of robins in the spring, a large band of Gypsies would come and camp on their way north. Papa allowed them to stay, but he was not exceedingly cordial. He worried about their fires, and usually found several tools missing from the barns after they left. Oftentimes chickens, and once even a new calf, disappeared. The children of Conway were fascinated by these strange, mysterious, free-roamers and looked forward to their arrival. But even now she could hear Mama's stern warning, "You stay out of the Gypsy Woods while those thieves are here!" And last night, Julia thought Mama's voice had sounded that same way.

Mae Henry could be seen more clearly now. From the road she moved slowly through the opening in the privet hedge into the backyard. She did everything slowly.

The house was quiet, but Julia knew Papa would be up drinking his coffee. He would let Mae Henry in, then go out in the little black two-seater Ford and check on a sick mule or some other problem on one of the farms. Later he would come back for breakfast. Soon the others would awaken to the smell of hot biscuits, grits, fried ham and coffee from the kitchen below.

The excitement Julia Sutherland felt over the arrival of this day was palpable. Leaving home this time seemed different, not like going off to boarding school or college, and she knew that she was nervous. She glanced around the room for items she might have forgotten to pack, and decided not to wait for Herbert, Mae Henry's husband, to come and lay a fire. She would dress quickly in the cold and finish packing, then he could take her trunk downstairs when he finished the milking.

As she dressed, she tried to remember if she had ever won an argument with Mama. Julia decided that last night she had not handled herself well. She remembered Miss Standard in Debating Club saying, "If you lose your temper, you have lost the debate." She had lost her temper, and purposely trying to hurt her mother, she had said bitter things. Things like, "Mama, you have always loved George and William more than us girls. You have always let them go anywhere they wanted to go, and do whatever they wanted to do. You have never refused them anything and you've always given them the best! You have never tried to understand me. You just want me here to help you with the housework and the sick." She remembered now that the sharp, biting words had felt good to say. "Until I went off to boarding school, I didn't even know a chicken had *white* meat."

Mama had not replied.

"Well, I don't care how you feel, nothing is going to stop me. I am going!"

There had been many arguments over the last several weeks, and last night, while Julia was packing, Mama had come upstairs. She usually came upstairs only on Saturday mornings to inspect the housekeeping of the bedrooms.

She had stood in the doorway watching Julia pack. The waves of warm, brown hair that framed her face were beginning to show a little gray. The usual softness around her eyes and mouth was missing, as was the softness in her voice.

"Julia, I am going to tell you one more time, I do not want you to go! How can you even consider going off to some God-forsaken place to teach, 150 miles away? There's a war going on, sickness everywhere. You are not even certified!"

Anger and hurt had spilled out an answer and the argument began. "Mama, you went 'way off' from Atlanta to Conway to teach--and you met Papa."

"That was different. Does this family mean nothing to you?"

Julia did not answer for a moment.

"I'm not going to Alaska, Mama. Chalk Creek is still in Georgia."

"Don't you use that tone of voice with me, young lady!"

Julia bit her lip. "Chalk Creek has had no teacher, no one, since October. I want to feel useful. In French class Dr. Tidwell told us, 'You girls of privilege have a responsibility, an obligation if you will, to humanity.' Something about *noblesse oblige,* and I do feel this Mama. Besides, there is nothing to do here in Conway. I feel like I am in prison."

"I am sure that you are aware that every single member of the Banks family is sick with influenza. And since his wife died with it at Christmas, Mr. Park could use some help with those four little girls---if you, Miss Sutherland, are so anxious to serve humanity."

Mama's sarcasm was like a tearing pain in Julia's chest, but she was determined not to succumb.

"Mama, you just don't understand. I've rolled bandages, and I've sold more Liberty Bonds than anyone else in the county. Papa won't hear of me going anywhere with the Red Cross."

Julia knew she sounded angry, but she did not care. "All the boys are either already in France or in training camp. They even took Will Lewis, slew-footed as he is. Can't you see, I want to do something important? I don't care how you feel, nothing is going to stop me. I am going!"

Julia watched as her mother drew a long, deep breath. Her teeth were set tightly, her chin raised. Her steel eyes narrowed and seemed to probe Julia like a surgeon's scalpel. Her countenance was that of total disapprobation. She seemed to struggle for control. In a barely audible whisper, the acrid words came. "You are right. I do not understand you. I think I shall never understand you."

"Mama, you are not listening to me! You refuse to hear what I am saying! I am suffocating here."

"And you are not listening to me, Julia Sutherland. If you were, you would hear me telling you that your own family needs you. You are not honoring your father and your mother. You are willful and selfish."

These words stung Julia like a cutting whip. She knew well the Biblical command, but she was struggling against her own need for independence. Julia did not blink but looked steadily into her mother's face. No other words were spoken.

Silence stood between them like an ugly conglomerate stone wall made equally of parental frustration and youthful self-will. Abruptly Mama turned and left the room.

Anger, resentment, resolve, perhaps a little anxiety, emotions that Julia did not fully comprehend, and did not want to feel, swept over and warred within her. Her chin quivered.

Later that night, through their closed bedroom door, Julia heard Mama talking loudly, angrily to Papa. She had never heard anything like this before. Mama always called her husband "Mr. Sutherland", and he referred to his wife, twelve years his junior, as "Miss Susie". Julia had seen Papa kiss Mama on many occasions and for all their formality, she knew there was love and respect between them. He even called her "Susie" when he thought they were alone.

The line of demarcation between the house and the farms was distinctly drawn. Mama was master of the house, the yard, the flower and vegetable gardens, and the cow barn. Papa never interfered. Her word was law. If she said she needed two men, mules and plows for the vegetable garden next week, they were provided. His domain was the farms.

Julia heard Mama saying, "Mr. Sutherland, why don't you do something? You have not said one word to Julia about her leaving. Why don't you stop her? You haven't really forced her to give up this idea of leaving."

"Susie, there comes a time when..."

"She's being impossibly selfish--and you, you haven't done one thing to help."

"Not selfish, Susie. She's been sick and in bed all fall. Perhaps she's just restless."

"No. She's willful."

Julia didn't want to hear anymore. She would never convince her mother that she wasn't being selfish. Since appendicitis had kept her in bed for six weeks last fall, she had not been able to return to college. As she closed her door, Julia said under her breath, "I am Not being selfish!"

The name of the newspaper read, *The Atlanta Journal*. In smaller print were the words "Covers Dixie like the Dew". It arrived from Atlanta daily by train. Julia remembered that it was early November, that Papa had put the paper down on the floor by his chair. This indicated he had finished it. No one sat in Papa's chair in the back living room, and no one bothered the paper until he put it down. The classified advertisement section happened to be on top. Out of curiosity, Julia searched the ads for anything unusual. Presently, it seemed to jump out at her in bold type.

Acme Teacher Agency. WANTED: Young ladies in good health, of high moral caliber, free to travel to areas needing teachers. some college required.

Send application to: P. O. Box 1154, Atlanta, Georgia.

To travel---visions of meeting a gallant young man on horseback immediately came to mind. Julia slipped that section of the paper out and carried it to her room.

She was thinking that if she discussed this plan with Mama and Papa they would emphatically say, "No." She might not be accepted by the agency, so she would say nothing about her plans yet.

Her application was very simple: three years at Buford College, boarding school before that. The three- dollar fee to join the agency seemed excessive and would deplete her savings, but if it would mean a job, then it would be worthwhile.

Two weeks passed and she heard nothing from her application. In a rather sarcastic manner she wrote to them again saying, "If you have no openings in Middle Georgia or North Georgia or in the entire United States, what about Europe, Irope or Orope?"

Immediately she received notification of the need for a teacher in Chalk Creek, Georgia. Julia had never heard of Chalk Creek. She found it, a tiny dot on the map, southeast of Macon, approximately 150 miles from Conway.

She sent her acceptance letter. Then she announced her plans to Mama and Papa and Judson became ill.

She tried to suppress the guilt she had allowed Mama to make her feel over her intention to leave, while Judson, only three, was so sick. Guilt was not a familiar emotion to Julia, and she did not like it.

Judson's little bed usually stayed in her room, but because Dr. Minter was coming to see him every day, Mama had Herbert move it into their room downstairs. Many families in Conway had at least one member dangerously ill with influenza. Dr. Minter had said on one of his visits, that there were enough cases in the county to call it an epidemic.

"Did you know, Susie," he had asked, "that Italian astrologers thought 'influenza' was caused by the 'influence' of heavenly bodies, and they gave it the name?"

"It was no heavenly body that caused this ailment," she countered. "The Devil himself thought this one up!" Mama, with her love for Greek, thought "pandemic" a better term. "It's like an evil wind that can't be seen and can't be stopped."

For over a week Judson had a very high fever and a croupy cough that racked his little body. As they fashioned a tent over his bed with a broom handle and the bedspread, Dr. Minter continued, "It's already killed millions in Europe and Asia, Susie, and the only treatment we know is aspirin and fluids. It's a dastardly plague. It takes a long time to recover and relapses are frequent."

Mama had placed a small kerosene stove close to the bed. She would boil Vicks salve and water in a kettle and direct the steam under the covers of the tent. For a while, Judson's cough would improve. In spite of the frigid weather, they would open the windows and let in fresh air.

"I am very worried, Roger. Is it true that over in Waresville they have had as many as five to fifteen deaths a day?" Mama asked.

"That's right. They're just using a wagon to pick up the bodies. They're burying 'em in pine boxes and plan to have funerals later. In one family I've seen, the ten year old daughter is the only person able to care for the others."

Mama told Dr. Minter that George's letters from France often mentioned the large numbers of his division who were dying with influenza.

Julia thought it strange that with a war raging all around him, Mama seemed to worry more about her son sleeping in the cold mud and eating out of tins than she did about the Germans shelling the trenches.

Her thoughts of George and Judson were interrupted by the sound of Herbert's slow trudging up the stairs. Without his familiar whistling, it seemed unusual. He always whistled. His trademark songs were <u>Blessed Assurance</u>, <u>Jesus Is Mine</u> and <u>Amazing Grace</u>. When he was trimming the privet hedge or bringing the milk in from the cow barn or helping Mama in the flower garden, the familiar strains of these hymns carried by his powerful whistling could be heard clearly even inside the house.

He came into her room carrying a full coal scuttle, added to it the few lumps that were left in the scuttle on the hearth, then knelt to shovel the ashes into the empty scuttle. As he worked, he said, "We gonna' miss you, Mis' Juya."

"Oh, I'll miss you too, Herbert, but I am so excited."

"Mis' Susie, she seem right upsot about yo' goin'."

"Mama is very angry with me, Herbert. Her boys can go off to the University---even to France to fight a war---that's alright, but I can't go anywhere or do anything but work right here!"

"Well now, Mis' Juya, you been off to school and.."

"Oh, Herbert, Buford is not 'off', it's little more than fifty miles from here---it's like a women's prison. Mama came here to teach, why can't she understand that I want to try something new? Anyway, I'll be home in June when school's out."

"Yes'm, but that do seem like a right long time."

He finished shoveling the last of the ashes into the scuttle, stood and turned to leave. Julia knew immediately that something was wrong. His face was ashen and his eyes were scary wide.

"Herbert, something's wrong. What's the matter?"

"Oh, Mis' Juya, please Mis' Juya, please don't tell Ol' Miss! I'll talk to Cap'n Bill."

"Tell me, Herbert, what is it? What's happened?"

"Mis' Juya," Herbert took a quick breath, "I was milkin' this mawnin' and that lil' ol' new calf, that'un yo' Mama

11

loves, kepa nudgin' and a push'n and try'n to git in front of me to them tits," another quick breath, "I pushed him away, and yelled at 'im, and pushed him away again and again and finally I picked up a shubel, and with de flat side I jes tapped him up side the head, and Mis' Juya, that calf,---he fell over dead! Mis' Juya, please don't tell ol' Miss. I'll tell Cap'n Bill."

"I won't, Herbert, I promise I won't tell her."

Most of the hands seemed to feel this way. They all called him "Cap'n Bill", all except Doll. She was Mae Henry's grandmother and very old. She had been Papa's nurse when he was a baby and the only one who ever called him "Billy". Each time she came to the house, which was not often now, she would say in her high, thin voice, "Billy, don'cha ever forgit, you was bon'd de year de Yankees cumb'd, 18 and 64."

Mama, on the other hand, was respected, but she could be a hard taskmaster. She expected things to be done well, and often said, "I can see no excuse for carelessness or shiftlessness. 'Life is real and life is earnest'."

Julia could understand Herbert's reluctance to confess to Mama his mistake.

She put her hair brush in the trunk, closed it, and went downstairs.

When Mae Henry put Julia's plate of ham, grits and eggs in front of her, Julia heard her muttering, "Herbert didn' have no call to hit that lil' calf so hard. Mis' Susie's got enough troubles right now. She didn' need no more."

As her large body moved toward the kitchen, she added, "Sometimes I gits s'mad with Herbert I could jes kill him------and tell Jesus he died." Julia smiled. She would miss these two people.

Returning her empty plate to the kitchen, Julia put her arms around Mae Henry and hugged the familiar, soft body of this woman who had counseled her for as long as she could remember.

"Mae Henry, should I go? Mama is furious with me and Judson seems no better. What should I do? Should I go?"

"Mis' Juya," Mae Henry hesitated for a moment, then said, "sometimes when we feel we gotta do something, we just gotta go on and do it-----it don't matter what."

Julia looked deep into the eyes of this kind woman then kissed her warm, brown cheek, hugged her again and whispered, "Thank you, Mae Henry, thank you."

As she left the kitchen Julia turned, smiled and said, "But just because you feel you've got to kill Herbert, please don't do it."

Mae Henry's laugh bubbled up from somewhere deep inside. "No'm, I guess not."

In the large downstairs bedroom a low fire was burning in the fireplace grate. When Julia went in to tell him good-bye, Mama was sitting by Judson's bed feeding him some thin chicken broth and softly singing to him. Julia recognized the familiar words of the old Irish ballad Mama often sang in happier times.

> Kay mo ki mo
> do re wa, Hide my hoe
> and in step
> Sadie sing lum time
> some time Pattie wy.
> Link tum nip cap
> Kitchee kitchee ki me o.

Judson's flushed face and dull, listless eyes frightened Julia. She touched his forehead with the back of her fingers and quickly took them away. He was extremely hot. He did not smile nor seem to notice her. When Mama pressed the spoon to his lips he automatically sucked a tiny swallow of the broth.

Julia realized she had not grasped how dangerously sick he was. To herself she whispered, "Please God, let him live." And then louder, "Mama, will he live?"

Mama did not answer. She did not look at Julia. As her daughter leaned down to kiss her cheek, she turned her head away and breathed a quick and curt, "Good-bye."

Hot tears blinded Julia and she turned and left the room.

She moved into the breakfast room not wanting Mama to see her tears. The searing pain of rejection mingled with resentment within her. Her chin quivered and the room blurred.

Unaware of anything around her except the pounding of her heart and the confusion of her mind, Julia stood staring through the breakfast room, down the long hall to the stairway on the right. She knew that if she climbed the steps and returned to her room this pain in her chest would go away, and Mama would smile again.

Papa had already gone out to get the automobile.

As if on cue, the sound of Mae Henry softly humming came through the open door from the kitchen. Julia hesitated, listened for a moment, picked up her pocketbook, turned and went out the back door.

A war was raging in Europe, and a war of wills was raging within this house.

Chapter 2--The Journey

The fog had lifted to tree-top level as Papa slowly turned the big, green Studebaker into the long driveway. Herbert and Mae Henry, wiping her eyes with an apron corner, were watching and waving from the back yard. With an intuitiveness born out of years of silent observation, Mae Henry knew when anything was amiss within the family. She did not like friction or unhappiness, especially at a time of departure. She considered it bad luck. Julia's little sister, Mildred, who had begged Papa to let her go to the train, was waving at them from the car.

Before the curve in the driveway, Julia looked back at the big white house standing silently in the fog. She hoped it would always be there--gracious, secure, hospitable. The slight rise on which it stood had been known in the distant past as Hard Head. The old folks said that the name came from the time when early settlers and Indians met under the trees to barter, and tied their mules there.

Papa liked to tell visitors, "Sometime after 1821, when the treaty with the Creek Indians was signed and this land was opened to the white man, my grandfather came here in a covered wagon with his wife and two sons, and settled near a bold spring. This house started as a four room cabin."

Now the place was known as Hillcrest. Two-story Doric columns supported the roof of the wide front porch, which wrapped around both sides of the house.

On the porch were several large white rocking chairs, and an inviting swing hung securely on chains. Julia thought of the many hours she, George and Ruth had spent as children trying to keep all the chairs rocking at once, or playing "train" on the swing. Last summer she and Charles Lawton had sat there and watched for Venus to appear in the evening sky. He held her hand and told her of his ambition to become a dentist. One night he had pulled her close to him and kissed her. Charles was now lying in a hospital somewhere in France. His mother called it shell shock.

There was not time now to dwell on this.

As they rode along, Julia asked, "Papa, why can't Mama understand my wanting to go---to do this? You understand, don't you?"

"Yes, I think I understand, Julia, and I trust you. I know this is something you feel you have to do, but we don't know anything about this place."

Papa slowed the automobile to allow a stray chicken to cross the road in front of them and then continued, "You know it is very hard for a lot of fathers to ever see their sons as grown men. I knew a man once who thought his fifty-year-old son was still too young for responsibility, to make his own decisions. I suspect, for some mothers it's difficult to realize their girls are ready to leave them. You don't have to go through with this you know. It's not too late to change your mind, even now." There was a hopeful, almost pleading quality in his words.

"I know, Papa, but I am going. I can't let the agency down, and besides, I think I shall love feeling independent. I wish Mama could understand."

"Well, if you don't like it, if it's not what you expected, all you have to do is write me and I'll send you the money to come home. It's five long months until June." Papa added with a smile, "If you had not been so sarcastic in your letter they might not have hired you."

"I know, Papa," she laughed. "It's always been one of my best developed qualities."

"We're going to miss you."

"I'll miss you too, and this little lady." Julia hugged the five year old sitting by her and said, "You'll have a birthday while I'm gone. Are you ready to be six years old?" Mildred smiled and nodded.

For a few minutes the three rode in silence. In the open fields on both sides of the road, brown rows of dead cotton plants stood shriveled and curled. Occasionally, an overlooked white fluff clung tenaciously to its boll. After the danger of frost was past, Papa would have these fields plowed, new seeds planted, and the cycle of chopping, blooming, weeding and picking would begin all over.

They passed the Bradley place on the right, and then on the left, the un-worked, weed covered fields of the McKemmie place. Papa said, "I saw Jake McKemmie yesterday. He suddenly seems thirty years older, and I don't believe Mrs. McKemmie has come out of the house or spoken to anyone since Clifford was killed. You know he was the future of the McKemmie farms." Julia remembered that Clifford had been called up in the first draft lottery in 1917 and had been in France only a few weeks.

Papa continued his musings. "You know small towns in Georgia seem to be of three kinds: those that were planned with streets laid out in gridiron fashion; or those with streets radiating from a central hub on which the Courthouse stands; or those, like Conway, that have grown up along a railroad line with the tracks bisecting the town."

Julia nodded.

As they passed the drugstore with Dr. Minter's office in the back, Julia noticed his shiny, new Maxwell standing out in front. While he made his house calls, Mrs. Minter would keep the drug store open. Where the wide dirt street in front of the J.M. Sutherland Company and the buggy works crossed the railroad track, the yellow clapboard depot stood. Two passenger trains and four freight trains passed through each day. Meeting the train was a social event, and a crowd usually gathered.

Julia's mouth suddenly felt dry, but her palms were wet. She did not want Papa to see how excited she was, and as the car stopped she managed to say with composure, "I love you, Papa. Thank you for letting me go. I wish Mama could do that, too."

Papa said nothing. Two men came over from the depot to help Papa with the trunk. Then he went inside and bought Julia's ticket. She must change trains in Griffin, then change again in Macon to the spur going to Chalk Creek. It would be late in the afternoon when she arrived.

Several people were milling about outside the depot, others were waiting in the post office or in wagons. A group of men in Story's Barbershop was watching from the big window to see who was leaving or arriving. The long, wailing whistle had sounded in the distance, probably at the Gypsy Woods. As Papa came back with her ticket, Julia thought, "There isn't much time."

At this moment Mr. Gist, the ticket agent, came running out of the depot in his shirt sleeves, suspenders showing, waving a small package.

"Miss Julia, Miss Julia," his heavy breathing made small white clouds in the air, "I almost forgot. Miss Janie brought this by for you early this morning. It's something she said was important for you to have."

"Oh, thank you, Mr. Gist." Julia's words were drowned by the noise of the approaching train.

He took her outstretched hand in his free one, handed her the package and said earnestly, "We're really going to miss you, Miss Julia." He turned and was gone.

Julia hugged Papa, kissed Mildred's cheek, got on the train and walked quickly down the aisle. She found an empty seat on the station side, slid the back of the seat so that she could face forward and settled in by the window.

Outside, a brisk wind whipped the lapels of the conductor's black jacket. A few rays of sunshine reflected from the celluloid cover on the bill of his cap and glinted in Julia's eyes as she pressed her face close to the glass. She waved again to Papa standing below her on the station platform, and blew a kiss to Mildred. Her tiny hand seemed lost in Papa's large one.

"How ramrod straight he holds that tall, thin, six-foot-two inch frame!" Unexpectedly, she felt tears welling in her eyes. She wondered if there were tears in Papa's eyes, too. He was wearing his dark Sunday coat and a black felt hat. In summer it would be a Panama straw and the black string tie he wore in every season.

Now the conductor was struggling to assist plump Mrs. Oxner from the metal step to the train step. With her thick coat, fur neck piece, two large paper sacks and her hand bag, it was difficult to find an elbow to hold. Three round hatboxes had already been put in the baggage car with her trunk. Julia knew that Mrs. Oxner was going to Atlanta to help her daughter, whose children had influenza. She was in no mood to share her seat with this talkative woman, and was grateful that just as Mrs. Oxner started down the aisle, the train lurched forward and Mrs. Oxner took the first available seat.

A sudden loud hiss of steam from under the train frightened Mildred. Julia watched Papa lift her into his arms, drying her tears. The train never stopped long in Conway. With what seemed to be one movement, the conductor stooped to pick up the metal step, called sharply, "All board-t", and swung himself aboard. As the train began to gather speed, Julia's excitement and anticipation far outweighed any sadness she felt at leaving Mama, Papa, and home.

She waved to Papa as long as she could, but it only took a moment for the train to pass the barber shop, the Masonic Lodge and the post office, and they were gone.

From the men's room behind her, strong smelling cigar smoke curled upward. Julia took off her navy blue suit coat, settled back and determined she was not going to let anything bother her. She had struggled too hard to get here. Papa had said she would only have thirty-five minutes to change trains in Griffin. She must check on her trunk and be sure that it was transferred to the Macon line. She did not want anyone to guess that this was her first time traveling alone. Papa had warned her not to talk to strangers.

"Don't ask questions of anyone except the ticket agent. Do you understand?"

"Yes, Papa, I understand," she had replied, adding with a smile, "won't everyone in Chalk Creek be a 'stranger' at first? Weren't you a stranger at first to Mama?"

"You know what I mean," Papa concluded sternly.

Many times Julia had heard the story of the day Mama and Aunt Nanny first came to Conway in 1894, Aunt Nanny to teach elocution and mathematics, Mama to teach Latin and Greek. Mama still enjoyed reading her Bible in Greek.

"Everyone in town knew the new teachers were arriving that day." Mama's eyes would sparkle and narrow a bit as she remembered. Julia loved hearing her tell the story.

"When we stepped off the train from Atlanta, near the station platform was a tall, immaculately-dressed man sitting on a large, roan horse. Beside him stood a shiny, black surrey hitched to a sleek, black horse. The gentleman removed his hat, bowed, and gallantly offered his surrey and man, Henry, to drive us to the Dormitory, where all the unmarried teachers lived."

"And the gentleman turned out to be Papa!" Ruth would always squeal at this point. Three years younger than Julia, and never able to keep a secret, she delighted in making this announcement to whomever was hearing the story for the first time.

The conductor interrupted Julia's reverie as he came down the aisle calling, "Tickets please." Julia glanced up and saw Mrs. Oxner waving to her. Julia nodded, then quickly looked down and picked up the small package Mr.Gist had handed her. Unwrapping it she found a thin volume entitled, <u>What A Young Girl Ought to Know</u>, published in 1905. The first pages revealed that this book was "commended by" no less than eleven stern faced ladies whose pictures had titles such

24

as "Eminent American Temperance Worker" or "Eminent Canadian Temperance Worker". More than a million copies in English had been sold.

> It was dedicated "to the thousands of girls
> whose honest inquires concerning the origin
> of life---deserve such a truthful answer as
> will enable them to avoid vice, and deliver
> them from solitary and social sins."

Smiling, Julia thought, "Even reading this is better than listening to Mrs. Oxner enumerate the various illnesses of her grandchildren."

Flipping through the pages, she noted that the author wrote at length about flower seeds and planting them in the ground, and then bird eggs developing in the mother bird's body. The next chapter seemed to deal with the human body as a temple and the importance of correct posture. Papa had always told her, "Julia, don't slouch. Stand up straight. Hold your head high and look people in the eye. Remember, you are a daughter of God, the King."

This author was saying that it was vital for young girls to stand straight "for you are making the future little room in which your small child will live for three-fourths of a year." It never once informed the young girl how the egg in the "little room" was changed into the "small child". Scanning the rest of the book revealed to Julia the importance of table manners, polite conversation and not letting your eyes gaze on unworthy pictures or reading matter.

"Dear Miss Janie," Julia chuckled. "She must think I am on my way straight to perdition." Miss Janie was a spinster who lived at the dormitory, did sewing, and taught the high school girls' Sunday School class. Julia remembered Miss Janie always had bad breath. She tried to remember if she had ever seen Miss Janie smile. Papa often said, "Miss Janie's sense of humor is badly constipated," and Mae Henry's apt description was, "Mis' Janie, she got a lot of veenega in her face".

The train whistle shrilly interrupted Julia's thoughts. The car door banged open and the conductor called, "Griffin". Black smoke and cinders came in through the open door. The thirty-five mile trip had taken an hour and forty-five minutes, including the stop at the big tank in Jolly to take on water.

A man behind her spoke loudly, "Barney Oldfield musta been driving this here engine today. We been a-goin' like sixty!"

The Union Depot, just completed four years ago, was a large brick building. Now as many as twenty trains came through daily carrying freight and passengers. Julia watched to see her trunk taken off the train and placed on a baggage cart to await the train to Macon.

At the far end of the depot was a frame building with a small sign over the entrance that said Depot Grill. The side of the building had been painted bright red. On this background, in large, swirly, white letters were the words

Refresh Yourself

Drink Coca-Cola   5 c in bottles

Relieves Fatigue

"Mama might not approve of my going in there," Julia decided, "but I'm thirsty and I think I'll try one."

The grill was smoky and noisy. All of the stools at the counter were filled with men. Just as she stepped inside the swinging door a man on the stool nearest her whirled around, spat on the floor a large mouthful of soup, and loudly shouted, "Blaze, god damn you!"

Julia changed her mind about the Coca-Cola and backed out of the door.

Inside the station, clusters of soldiers were standing, others leaned against the walls, some were sprawled on the wooden benches trying to sleep, a few were reading. Many more milled about outside. Julia threaded her way between the rucksacks and other army gear toward the ticket window to check on her departure time. She thought of Clifford McKemmie and wondered how many of these young men would not come home from the war. She kept her eyes discreetly downward avoiding eye contact, but she was aware of cat-calls and exclamations from the men.

"Awright!"

"Un-huh".

"Nice ankles".

"Yes-Ma'amm!"

She knew that Miss Janie would have been horrified, but Julia thought it was not entirely unpleasant.

She waited in front of the ticket window while the agent read his newspaper. Clearing her throat and saying, "Excuse me," several times, the agent finally looked at her.

"Troop train out of Atlanta be here at 2:10," he barked, "taking these men to Camp Wheeler at Macon. Three days ago, January 1st, President Wilson nationalized the railroads. That's how come your fare went up. Next train to Macon'll be behind the troop train. Y'luggage'll be put on it." His eyes abruptly returned to the paper.

"Well, thank you sir," Julia replied too sweetly. "It is evident that courtesy is not a requirement for your job!"

It was not necessary to speak to any more strangers.

As her train pulled out of the Griffin station, Julia looked over the tops of the trees and could see the head of the Confederate Soldier monument stoically facing North. She also noticed new street lights at regular intervals along the wide dirt street.

Two men sitting behind her were talking about the war, President Wilson, and the Germans.

"Well, you know, I b'leve the Germans is causing this influenza epedemic."

"Yeah, you might be right. Those British have lost a helluva lot of men from sickness and the war. I read over 400,000 just between July and November. I think we need to get more soldiers to'em."

She thought of her brother George, and wished he did not have to be one of those soldiers.

After about thirty minutes the train jerked to a stop and the conductor came through announcing the small town of, "Boling-broke, Bo-ling-broke".

A mountain-sized woman, who had boarded the train in Griffin and sat across the aisle facing Julia, erupted to her feet, spilling her shoe box of fried chicken and deviled eggs on the floor. She started down the aisle, stepping in the eggs and screaming, "The train's broke! Lord God, get me outta here. I know'd if I got on this train sumpin' would break---I tol' my son not to make me ride this thang---I know'd sumpin' would break."

The conductor tried to calm her. Julia tried not to laugh out loud. "Papa will love this story", she thought.

By mid-afternoon the train slowly pulled into Macon's Terminal Station, an enormous limestone structure that extended for two city blocks.

Julia remembered Papa telling her that this station had cost one million dollars to build in 1916. He had said, "As many as a hundred passenger trains a day come to Macon, plus the troop trains."

Outside her window she could see throngs of people hurrying in every direction. Baggage carts loaded with luggage lined the covered platform that stretched the length of the building. She wondered if her trunk would get on the right train.

Hundreds of soldiers, carrying heavy rucksacks, were either coming from or going to the infantry training center at nearby Camp Wheeler. Through the jostling crowd, Julia made her way inside the building. Once inside, it was hard not to stand and gawk. She had never seen such a building. The three story vaulted ceiling was supported by marble columns, and the walls of Georgia marble were topped by a carved marble frieze. "Is this what it is like, as the song writer said, to 'dwell in marble halls'?" she wondered.

A newsboy, with a canvas satchel of papers over his shoulder, pushed through the crowd hawking, "Telegraph, Macon Telegraph. Unmarried men to do nation's army fighting. New draft policy---only men without dependents to go to the trenches. Get your paper here! 5¢. Suffragettes face House Committee hearing. Telegraph." He was doing a brisk business.

Julia made her way to one of the four ticket windows. Each had a long line. A rather flamboyantly dressed middle-age man approached her and offered to take her money and get the ticket for her. Julia declined his offer. Not discouraged, from his place ahead of her in line he kept turning, and smiling and nodding at her. She tried to avoid his gaze and hoped this man was not going on the same train.

"Why on earth," she asked herself, "did I want to leave home and do this? What do I hope to accomplish?"

For an instant she wished that she, like Mildred, had Papa's big hand to hold.

With little time to spare Julia Sutherland boarded the train to Chalk Creek.

Chapter 3--The Arrival

An hour and fifteen minutes later, the conductor and Julia were waiting on the platform between cars as the train slowed. He held the metal step in his hand.

"How long you gonna stay in this place, ma'am? There's not much to it."

"Well, at least until June," Julia answered.

He shook his head as though he did not believe her. "Well--good luck, ma'am. We don't normally stop here, just put the mail sack, if there is any, on that hook."

He swung down from the train and placed the step on the dirt for her. Julia thanked him and watched to see that her trunk was lowered to the ground from the baggage car. There was no visible town. There was no depot. A sign designating an unpainted wooden,   three-sided shed as Chalk Creek, Georgia, hung from only one of the two chains that had originally held it. Julia wondered how long it had been so ignored and neglected.

No one was there to board, and no one was there to meet her. Already the train was beginning to move. The track curved to her right. Julia watched as, picking up speed, the train moved faster and disappeared into deep shadows and scrub pine. It was almost 5:30 and would be dark soon. Perhaps Papa was correct. She didn't have to do this.

Behind her, across the track and facing a narrow dirt road, Julia saw a small frame store. A sign over the front porch of the building read, "Hawkins General Store". A pole beside the building and a wire leading to it indicated a telephone. Julia noticed the distinct, sour smell of pigs. A screen door slammed and a tall woman clutching a long dark coat around her came out of the store. Hunched over against the wind she hurried along to a house down the road. She did not look toward Julia.

In a vacant lot next to the store, barely visible in the Johnson grass, sedge and weeds, stood several rusty hay rakes, an old wagon listing to one side for lack of wheels, and something Julia guessed might have been a hay mower at one time. Beyond the vacant lot three houses lined the road. They stood like triplets with similar front porches and Victorian fretwork. All needed paint. The woman entered the first of these. The road ended beyond the third house.

In front of Julia and across what appeared to be the main road was a small wooden building with a barber pole outside and a sign that read "Chalk Creek Post Office". This main road curved up a hill to the left and was lost in pine saplings. Several small houses dotted along both sides of the hill. The soil looked different, more sandy than loamy like Conway's and there were more pines than hardwoods. The only sign of life in Chalk Creek seemed to be the woman in a hurry and a big gray cat stretching and licking itself near the barber pole.

Standing there wondering what she should do, Julia began to hear lumbering and rattling sounds in the distance, sounds like that of a truck coming fast down a bumpy hill. The sounds did not prepare her for the reality. As it rounded the curve in a cloud of dust, for a moment she was not sure whether it was a wagon or a truck. With no roof and no sides, just a cracked windshield, and a pine plank for the front seat, it resembled a wagon with a motor. Spewing gravel, the truck stopped in front of her and three men quickly climbed down.

"I'm sorry we're late, ma'am," the shortest and oldest of the three spoke first. He was slender, wore glasses, and from ear to ear a fringe of white hair showed beneath his dark hat. As he spoke, a plug of tobacco moved up and down in one cheek. His friendly grin revealed several missing teeth. Julia guessed him to be in his mid sixties.

The second man, about forty-five, who was taller and looked as though he had a pillow stuffed in the front of his overalls, spoke. "We didn' mean to keep you waitin', ma'am, but I was a little late gittin' off at the Clay Company. We're the Budds."

Pointing to the first man he added, "He's my Pa, Big Budd, I'm known as Little Budd, and this here's m'son we calls Bitty Budd." Pointing to each one, he said again, "Big Budd, Lil' Budd and Bitty Budd."

Margaret M. Landham

The youngest Budd, about twenty-five, and largest of the three, shifted the match stick he held between his teeth, removed his gray knit cap, nodded his head and grinned. "Hello, ma'am." His left eye did not look in the same direction as his right and Julia found it hard to tell which one he was using. All three men wore overalls that were covered with fine white dust.

Little Budd, the spokesman, explained, "Ma'am, we gonna take you to stay with my cousin, Rose Wimbush, and her husband Clarence."

"Thank you," Julia said, smiling. She thought it strange that the principal or school superintendent had not come to meet her. Was she really supposed to go with these men? They seemed harmless enough and there was no other choice.

As the men put her trunk on the back of the truck, Julia noticed that Big Budd walked with a limp. Bitty Budd crawled in the back with the trunk and held it by the leather handle. She sat between Big Budd and Little Budd, who did the driving. The heavy odor of sweat surrounded her. The back of the seat still showed some evidence of black leather, and the wooden steering wheel had been mended in several places with rags and friction tape.

As the truck bounced over the rutted, narrow road, sending small rocks and dust in its wake, Julia clutched the splintery wooden seat with both hands. Her pocketbook kept sliding from her lap to the floor board. With a sweeping gesture, Little

Budd pointed to both sides of the road and said something she could not distinguish above the rattling of the truck.

Bitty Budd shifted the match stick again, leaned forward from the back and shouted into Julia's ear, "Pa said Mr. Northrup, he owns this land 'long here, both sides the road'."

"That's nice," Julia nodded, teeth clinched.

"Mr. Northrup," Bitty Budd continued, "he's Superintendent of the Clay Company and Timekeeper."

Julia thought it was too difficult to force conversation, but in an effort to appear sociable she shouted, "Does Mr. Northrup live in Chalk Creek?"

"Yes'm." This time Little Budd answered. "Most of the time he's around, to keep an eye on things at the mine--you can't see his house from the road. It's up a ways behind them trees."

Pines and scrub hardwoods were thick along both sides of the road. Occasional outcroppings of rock could be seen in the few sandy-looking fields, but there were no large vistas of open planted fields as she was accustomed to seeing. Mama would have said, "This land looks too poor to burn."

Little Budd continued, "It's been bitter cold all day."

Julia noticed that hoarfrost still clung to clumps of dead goldenrod and turned the banks of the road white.

Bitty Budd leaned close again, "We're right lucky it ain't rained since Tuesday. After a big rain this road kin be slick as glass."

Julia nodded and wondered how much farther they were going. She wanted to ask if slick was worse than washboard bouncy, but just at that moment the right front tire found a deep hole that sent her pocketbook again to the floor. Big Budd smiled and retrieved it for her once more. As they bounced along she wondered if Chalk Creek might be the "Irope" or "Orope" she had sarcastically referred to in her application follow-up letter, or perhaps more likely, this place is "end of rope". The contrast between this experience and Mama's arrival in Conway twenty-five years ago seemed comical. Papa will love this story, she thought.

A small plowed field came into view on the left. About twenty rows of last year's corn stalks stood brown and neglected, but it was the first sign of farming she had seen. A cloud of blackbirds suddenly descended on the stubble. The road forked and Little Budd took the right.

Big Budd leaned out, spat, and shouted, "It's jes' up ahead now."

The road curved, the truck slowed and a rusty sign attached to a four-by-four post announced that they had arrived at the Wimbush place.

A weak sun cast long shadows on a clean swept dirt yard. In the center of the clearing stood a small, unpainted frame house, supported at each corner by a stack of rocks. Smoke was rising from a narrow, square brick chimney. Little Budd parked the truck under a large chinaberry tree near the right side. Back of the house Julia could see a fenced chicken yard, a wood pile, and a path partially obscured by a few small pines. She assumed it led to the privy.

Two blue tick hounds crawled out from under the house loudly barking and announcing visitors. The front door opened and a tall, raw-boned woman with gray-brown hair pulled tightly behind her ears stepped onto the sagging front porch. She could be anywhere from thirty-five to sixty, Julia thought.

She was wearing a thin sweater over a flowered calico dress, and a pair of men's felt bedroom shoes. She did not smile. With her arms folded firmly, holding the sweater across her chest and her eyes squinting against the wind, Julia thought this surely could be a portrait entitled, "Reluctant Hospitality".

The cold breeze whipped at Julia's skirt and she felt chilled to the bone. Bitty Budd lifted her trunk from the truck.

"We brung ya' the new teacher, Rose." He grinned and snickered, "She sho' is prettier than the last 'un."

Julia wondered if the porch would support more than three of them at once. A boy of about eleven, dressed in overalls and a flannel shirt, and a girl, perhaps nine, came around the side of the house. No one made introductions so Julia spoke, "How do you do? I am Julia Sutherland."

"Un huh." The tall woman rubbed her hands on her dress. "My name's Rose, Rose Wimbush, and these here is my cheerun', Sari and Donny." Her voice seemed a bit hostile, suspicious, Julia thought.

Turning and smiling at the two, Julia replied, "Hello." Donny ducked his chin and pushed on a rock with the toe of his boot.

Sari asked shyly, "Is you gonna' teach us for awhile?"

"I'd like to try," Julia answered.

"Yawl wanna' come on in, its been kindly cold today." Rose spoke slowly. She pushed on the heavy plank door studded with rusty nails and held it open for Julia to step inside.

Little Budd and Bitty Budd brought in Julia's trunk. "Where ya' want'm to put this thang, Rose?" Big Budd asked.

Julia quickly glanced around the sparsely furnished room. An iron double-bed had been arranged in one corner, covered with a faded pastel quilt. A straight chair was on either side and a chifforobe stood nearby. Two rocking chairs faced the fire place in the center wall. A rough plank served as a mantel and held three kerosene lamps. Two straight, caned-bottom chairs stood on either side of a small square table under the front window. The unpainted rough walls extended only about seven feet high, leaving the rafters exposed. Through an opening to the right of the fireplace Julia could see part of the kitchen. There were no rugs on the unpainted plank floors.

Rose pointed toward a narrow hall on the left and the opening to what would be Julia's room. The men put her trunk inside and backed out of the small space. There were no inside doors in the house. A thin, green flowered cloth that could be pulled across the doorway on a tight wire offered her room a little privacy. A single bed stood against the inside wall near the doorway.

"This'll be your bed, Mis' Sutherlan'. Is that right, Sutherlan'?"

"Yes, Mrs. Wimbush, but you may call me Julia."

"Well, this here's a new cotton mattress. It sets on coil springs. Me and Clarence ordered 'em from Sears and Roebuck jes' before Mis' Potter came. I don't know how long it'll last. Lil' Budd's Ma, she helped me make our corn husk 'uns. She said they'd last more n' twenty-five years. I reckon so, 'cause they's still good after fifteen years."

Julia appraised the tiny room. Underneath the one small window was a three drawer oak chest with a bowl and pitcher on the top. Hanging inconveniently to the left of the window was a cracked, unframed mirror. Rose pointed to the chest, "That top drawer's empty, Mis' Sutherlan'. Mis' Potter's things is in the other two."

"I assume Miss Potter was the former teacher, Mrs. Wimbush. Do you mean she left her clothes here?"

"Oh yes'm," Rose said. "Clothes, books---she didn' take nuthin' 'ceptin' the clothes and coat she was a-wearin' when she went to school that day. She didn' let on to nobody that she's thinkin' 'bout leavin'. She also left without pay'n me for two weeks board."

"That's really very strange," Julia said, "Unfortunate."

"Well, I tol' Mr. Northrup, he's chairman of the school board, I tol' him, I ain't keepin' no more Yankee teachers, and that's final."

Prejudice dies hard, Julia thought. Aloud she asked, "Where was her home?"

"Some place in Pennsylvan'a, I think. She talked a lot about her boyfriend. He was from somewhere 'way off, I think she said Philadelfus. Anyhow, he didn' like her workin' way off down here. I figga he jes' come and got her." The angry tone was there again.

"Did anyone see him?" Julia pressed.

"No'm, nobody remembers seein''em."

"Well, what about her parents?"

"Oh--she tol' me 'bout them. They been dead for years. She didn' have no fam'ly. I think that's how come she tried t'please this boy-friend s'much. She didn' wan ta loose him, too."

"Well, it does seem she could have settled her rent and said good-bye."

Rose had opened the door to the dark-veneered chifforobe. It stood against the partition that separated this room from the sitting room. She was shifting dresses and shoes down to one end.

"She may have thought these clothes would pay for her board, but I can't wear nun of 'em. I'm gonna put on the grits now fa' supper. You kin git cha things unpacked. The school board members'll be here about eight o'clock, and the cheerin'll bring ya some water fa ya pitcher afta awhile. The path to the outhouse is out back. If the door's open nobody's in there."

"Thank you Mrs. Wimbush."

Julia's trunk was standing in the middle of the floor. Three nails for clothes protruded from the back wall, but there was barely enough room to walk between the bed and this wall. Perhaps, she thought, I could move the chest to make room for the trunk and leave my clothes hanging in it.

She was not sure now that they were appropriate for Chalk Creek, but Julia was proud of her clothes. Hanging inside the trunk was a brown, double-breasted coat suit, two tweed pleated skirts, a black straight skirt, several middy blouses, some with red sailor ties and some with navy ties, a gray crepe Sunday dress and coat, and a beautiful beige, lace-covered satin party dress with a pink ribbon bow at the neck. The shoe space held two new pairs of black and gray leather shoes. The pull-down tray revealed a mirror and tiny drawers for jewelry, hat pins, hair combs, and other small items. The three large drawers with their glass knobs were filled with undergarments Miss Janie had completed for her.

Across the dark narrow hall from her doorway was the opening to the kitchen. She could hear the plop, plop, plop of grits being stirred and smell ham frying, then came the sound of boots stamping and scraping on steps in back, and a man's voice asking, "Teacher come?"

"Un huh," Rose answered. "She's here, Clarence."

After supper Rose brought Julia a piece of brown paper. "Mis Sutherlan', maybe you could take and wrap up some of them things of Miss Potter's and put 'em under the bed. That'ud give you a little more room."

It seemed strange to be sharing this tiny room with someone who was no longer there. Julia decided to tackle the bottom drawer first. The little oak chest was rather rickety and the drawers were difficult to open.

Miss Potter's clothes were neatly folded and organized in stacks of blouses, underwear, nightgowns and stockings. The middle drawer contained many small items: a box of powder, hair combs, toilet water, a cameo pin, handkerchiefs, a fountain pen, ink bottle, a leather stationary folder, and a silver heart shaped locket on a long silver chain. Inside the locket was the picture of a Union officer. Julia debated about opening the folder. Curiosity won the debate. Inside, in a small, precise hand was an unfinished letter. Julia read,

"Dear Claire,

I have been busy here or I would have written to you sooner. This is a terrible place. You would not believe my living conditions. Everything is extremely primi- tive. I feel sorry for the children of this community, their parents are poor and they are far behind in their education. I shall be ever so glad to leave. You remember I told you that

Robert did not want me to come South, but I told him to leave me <u>alone</u> for this school year and then I would give him my answer. I believe he will.

There is something very strange , perhaps evil, about this"---

The letter abruptly ended.

That's odd, Julia thought. 'Evil'? Was she thinking of this family? This Community? What could she have meant by 'evil'?

Chapter 4--The Interview

Julia knew she was not sitting on a rocking chair but she felt as if the room was moving. None of the five school board members seemed to notice the swaying. For almost an hour now the questions had droned on. Perspiration beaded her forehead and she felt drops running down her spine. With her handkerchief she dared to blot her top lip.

The group had formed a circle with Julia's back to the fireplace. Stiff, austere Mr. Northrup, superin-tendent of the Clay Company, was chairman of the board. The power that accompanied this position appeared to be a heavy burden to him. His brow was deeply furrowed and he squinted above the small black, steel rimmed glasses that tightly pinched the end of his auger-like nose. He had already covered most of the basic questions: her age, education, background experience and family.

"Miss Sutherland," he continued, "we made a mistake in hiring Miss Potter. This must not happen again."

"No, sir."

"Of course we would prefer to have a man fill this position. But with the war going on---" He did not complete this sentence.

"You understand that you will be expected to teach reading, elocution, arithmetic, spelling, geography and history. I am interested in hearing what type of discipline you would use. Do you buy into that silly notion of the so-called educator, John Dewey, to do away with punitive punishment, or would you use the good ol' hickory stick?"

"Mr. Northrup, I believe I would try to let the punishment fit the crime, whenever possible."

He seemed satisfied with her answer.

Now Mrs. McCrane, sixtyish, leaned forward and asked, "Is you ever taught before, Miss Sutherland?"

"No, ma'am," Julia replied patiently, wondering if Mrs. McCrane had a hearing problem. She had answered this question already.

"Well, how come you choose Chalk Creek to teach at?"

"Mrs. McCrane," Julia cleared her throat, "I did not choose Chalk Creek. I applied to the Acme Placement Service for a teaching position, and they informed me that Chalk Creek had a position available."

"Uh, huh. Well, are you through goin' to school yet? Ya looks mighty young."

"No, ma'am. As I stated before, I have completed my junior year at college. I was ill with appendicitis last fall and couldn't go up and down steps for six weeks. It would have been difficult to make up that much lost time, so I chose to remain at home and seek a teaching position."

"Uh huh. Well, does thet mean thet you'll not be comin' back here next year? We needs a teacher that'll stay here and not leave. These here children have had so many different teachers they can't remember they names."

"I understand the problem, and I am sympathetic. At this time I am not certain exactly what I will do next fall." Julia was wondering if Miss Potter had to endure such a cross-examination when she came.

"Well, you know," Mrs. McCrane continued, "we pays real good. Thirty dollars a month ain't nothin' to sneeze at, especially since you ain't licensed n'all, and Mrs. Wimbush here, and all the others where you'll be stayin', they jes charges ya fifty cents a day for room and board. You kin come out mighty good!"

"Do you mean that I will move to different homes in the community?"

"Yes, Miss Sutherland, that is our policy," Mr. Northrup said. He was once again taking control. "You will start off here with this family. Then another family will invite you to move in with them. The charges are the same."

With an authoritative air and hostility in her voice, Sarah Hawkins said, "We do not want a repeat of Miss Potter's behavior. You are very young---just eighteen. Tell this board about your suitors."

Julia stared at her. Sarah Hawkins was a large woman who seemed to wear a permanent frown. Rose had told Julia that the only store in Chalk Creek was owned by Sarah and her husband, Jimmy. Julia recognized her as the woman she had seen in the dark coat.

Mr. Hawkins' eyes never left his wife, and each time she had spoken he had smiled and nodded in agreement. He was very thin and sat with both feet flat on the floor and with his knees and feet held firmly together. His slender hands formed a nest in his lap. It was not hard to guess who really ran Hawkins Store.

Julia wanted to reply, "I have ten suitors, all with horns and long red tails." But she remembered Papa's admonition about sarcasm, and she knew these people were taking their responsibilities very seriously. All she said was, "Mrs. Hawkins, at this present time, I have no serious suitor."

Rose Wimbush was the fifth member of the board, and the only one with school-aged children. She did not ask any questions.

Mr. Northrup straightened, took a gold watch from his vest pocket, and was about to say something when the lights of an automobile brightened the small front window. "That would be Mr. Marshall," he said. "Forty-five minutes late."

Rose opened the door and greeted Mr. Marshall. He was of average height, about forty Julia guessed, a well built man with sandy, wavy hair and watery blue eyes. Neatly dressed in a dark suit, he wore no hat. Julia thought he looked rather pale. She rose. Mr. Northrup introduced her to Gilbert Dudley Marshall, the School Superintendent of Holmes County Schools, all three of them, and ex-officio member of the Board.

"I am delighted to meet you, Miss Sutherland," Mr. Marshall said. "I apologize for my tardiness. I was meeting with one of the problem girls over in Kellston." Shaking his head, he added, "She can be a handful."

For Mr. Marshall's benefit, Mr. Northrup briefly reviewed the pertinent information that the board had covered. While the chairman talked, Mr. Marshall's eyes never left Julia. She felt them darting north, south, east and west, examining and scrutinizing every detail of her person. It made her feel somewhat uncomfortable and she tried not to notice, to avoid his gaze by looking at Mr. Northrup. By now, she thought, the superintendent must know her shoe size.

When the review was completed, Mr. Marshall kindly asked, "Do you have any questions you would like to ask us, Miss Sutherland?"

"Yes, I do," Julia replied. "Approximately how many children should I expect, what are their ages, what is the length of the school day?"

Mr. Northrup answered, "Eighteen children will be the maximum in attendance, Miss Sutherland, and they range in age from six to eighteen, in grades one through eight. The day begins at 8:30 and ends at 3:30. The salary depends upon the average attendance."

"I would imagine," Mr. Marshall said, "that twelve to fifteen probably will be the maximum number. Even though the Georgia Legislature passed the Compulsory Attendance Law two years ago, it is not strictly enforced and some children are needed to help with planting or harvesting crops. Anyway, if all the children came every day there would not be enough desks. As it is, many of the younger ones share a desk." Shaking his head, he added, "Miss Potter expressed to me her feeling that our school was far behind the Northern ones."

"And what is the primary occupation of the men in Chalk Creek?" Julia asked.

"The poor soil around Chalk Creek makes it virtually worthless for farming," Mr. Northrup said. "However, under this sorry land there is a fine white clay that is used in pottery and china and in coating certain papers. Almost all of the able-bodied men in this area are employed by the Clay Company. It is hard work, but steady employment. There is a small sawmill operation, but they only need a few men."

"I see," Julia nodded.

The questions had been answered, Mr. Northrup adjourned the business meeting, and Rose passed around a small peach basket filled with parched peanuts.

Mrs. Hawkins was the last to leave. Lingering at the door, she turned to Julia and asked, "Miss Sutherland, I want to ask you a personal question. Your hair is unnaturally thick and lustrous. Do you wear a transformation?"

Julia hesitated, feeling that this was none of Mrs. Hawkins' business. "No ma'am, I tangle my hair on the sides with a comb and then smooth it over." Turning her head she added with a smile, "In the back it is twisted into a figure eight. The girls at school call them 'cootie garages'."

Mrs. Hawkins did not return her smile.

As Rose put the few chairs back in their proper place she muttered aloud, "I gets so prevoked with Mis' Hawkins. She's like some tall bowl of water thet sumpin' keeps stirrin'. I wanta tell her to jes' set it down and let it settle. There jus ain't no peace about her, ever. We all got troubles, I don't reckon nobody's free from'um. But Mis' Hawkins, she's like somebody thet decides every day to set down on her lil' handful of thorns. I don't think I ever remember her to jes plain enjoy sumpin'."

"Do they have grown children, Mrs. Wimbush?"

"No'm. Never did have none."

"Perhaps," Julia ventured, "Mrs. Hawkins would have been different if she had been blessed with children."

"I don't think so, Mis' Sutherlan'. She's jes like her insides is all dried up. I feel real sorry for Jimmy havin' to live with'er."

"Well, I don't suppose he has to, does he?" Julia asked. "He could leave."

"I don't know who'd do his thinkin' fa' 'im if he went off."

Julia smiled.

They finished straightening the room and Julia asked, "When will Mr. Northrup let me know if I have been accepted by the board?"

"Well, Mis' Sutherlan', I don't reckon they've got a lotta choices right now. I 'spec you'll do."

"Mr. Marshall seems to be a very pleasent person," Julia said.

"Yes'm. He's a right fancy dresser alright. Always wearin' them shiny shoes. He do seem to like the cheerun."

During the interview Clarence, Sari and Donny had been sitting quietly in the kitchen. It was now bedtime so Clarence put two more logs on the fire, "to last a little longer," he said. Because the inside walls did not extend to the ceiling, the heat from the fireplace and the kitchen stove moved about and somewhat warmed the house. At least the heat lasted until the fires died out.

The open spaces also allowed sounds to carry and shadows to be reflected from the fire light.

Julia lay in bed thinking about the day and watching the red glow from the front room flickering on the ceiling. All at once she realized she was watching the silhouettes of Clarence and Rose as they undressed. Clarence, unhesitatingly, slipped off his suspenders and his shirt. Then sitting on the bed he untied and removed his boots. Julia heard them hit the floor. Standing again he removed his pants, placing them on the straight chair. He was now unbuttoning his BVD's and reaching under the bed for the slop jar. Julia heard him using it and then crawling into bed. During this time Rose had been removing her clothing under the tent of her flannel nightgown, which she had put on first. Julia felt as though she were peeping through a nonexistent key hole.

The shadows, however, were not as troublesome as the sounds that followed. She could have closed her eyes, but she could not seem to adequately stop up her ears. Their corn shuck mattress began to crackle and, for what seemed to be a long time, the bed rhythmically creaked and shook.

She knew that it was perfectly natural, but she was embarrassed, and felt that she was inside their room and there was no escape.

For several minutes she held the pillow over her head but it was suffocating. Eventually, it was over, and all was quiet. There had been no sounds from the children's room on the other side.

Julia's mind was so crowded with thoughts, she could not seem to complete one before another took over, and sleep was slow to come. She lay there wondering if Mama had thought of her today, whether she ever worried about her as she did about George. She thought of the unexpected strangeness of Chalk Creek and the people she had met. She wondered why she had wanted to leave home. The gulf that separated the comforts of her home from the sparseness of this one could be a million miles wide. Then she began to worry about herself.

"Will I be able to handle the challenge of teaching in a place like this, or will I, like Miss Potter, just give up and leave?"

Chapter 5--
The Wimbush Place

It was barely daylight when sounds from somewhere outside her small window penetrated the cocoon of sleep that had encompassed Julia. She realized it was Donny sing-songing loudly:

> *Sittin' on a kerbstone shootin' dice,*
> *I gits cooties, but you gits lice.*

Giggles were followed by laughter, and then it was Sari's turn as the singing got nearer.

> *My nose itches, yo' nose itches,*
> *Somebody's comin' with a hole in his britches.*

Both were laughing now, then suddenly Donny ordered. "Watch out, Sari, ya' spillin' it."

"I'm watchin'," she yelled. "Donny, sing 'I went to the river and I couldn't get across',"

"Hush up, you two," a gruff voice called from the back porch. "Teacher's still s-s-sleepin'." It was Clarence Wimbush, surprisingly stern in his admonition. Last night at supper Julia had thought he seemed quite patient and soft-spoken.

"Sorry, Pa," Donny answered. "We forgot about her."

Julia had groped her way to the window and watched, shivering, as the children crossed the yard from the road. Each of them carried two tin buckets suspended by ropes from the ends of small paddle-like yokes that fit around the back of their necks and across their shoulders. Carefully, and quietly now, they poured the fresh water into a large tin tank on the back porch.

"That'll do", Clarence said with shaving lather on his face. Clarence held a straight razor in one hand and a piece of broken mirror in the other. His enamel basin of water rested on the porch rail and a razor strop hung from a nearby nail.

From the kitchen Julia could smell coffee brewing and hear the plop, plop sound of Rose stirring grits. Saturday, January 5th, her first day in Chalk Creek had begun.

When they sat down for breakfast, Rose bowed her head and repeated a simple but sincere prayer. She finished by thanking the Almighty for the new teacher and asking for His blessings on her. Julia felt truly grateful for Rose's request. During the meal, which consisted of hot biscuits, sorghum syrup, grits, fried streak-of-lean, coffee, and milk for the children, there was very little conversation.

When Clarence did speak, Julia noticed an occasional stutter. She also noticed that his left arm seemed weak, almost useless and smaller than his right. As they were clearing away the dishes, Julia inquired about the churches in the area.

Rose said, "They won't be none this week, Mis' Sutherlan'. The nearest church, the one we goes to, is Shady Grove Baptist, over by Reedy Creek and it meets ever third Sunday. The Methodist Circuit preacher, he comes through ever second Sunday. They meets up at Piney Woods. So, they won't be no service tomorrow."

"I see," Julia said, "well is there something I can do to help you today, Mrs. Wimbush?"

Rose seemed startled. "No'm, I wouldn't think so, Mis' Sutherlan', but thank ya' for askin'." Then she added, "I'm jes' gonna put on a mess of turnip greens and later I'll make m'cornbread. Clarence may take Donny and go fishin' if it warms up, and Sari'll hep me wash these greens."

A cold wind stung Julia's cheeks as she carefully made her way down the path to the privy behind the chicken yard. Nothing different about this privy she thought---the usual two-holer with a smaller, lower one for the children. The fenced chicken yard, with only about eight chickens, was also home to three goats. Behind the goats was a good place for the privy, Julia decided. One odor pretty well canceled the other. The ground looked so sparse and sandy she thought the goats must be fed table scraps or share the chicken's cracked corn.

When Julia returned, Rose was on the back porch throwing out water from the turnip greens she had washed. They talked for a few minutes about the goats. "Yes'm, they're nice things to have. They not any trouble, they keep down the weeds and they don't smell bad like hawgs."

Julia wasn't too sure about that.

"That brown and white un's Nanny and the blackun's Billy. We calls that lil'un C'ly. You know they kin have as many as three kids in a year."

"Did you say C'ly?" Julia asked.

"Yes'm. She's they third kid. We jes raises'em to eat. We couldn't think up no good names and we didn' want the young'uns to git too attached to 'em. The first un was A, the next 'un B and this here one's C'ly. We'll probably kill her 'bout Easter time."

"I see. Well, you have a lot more name possibilities."

Rose did not seem to notice Julia's attempt at humor.

"Donny and Sari takes turns milkin' 'em. You like goat's milk, Mis' Sutherlan'? Nanny gives real rich milk."

"I'm sure I will learn to, Mrs. Wimbush."

"Well, that Mis' Potter, she never could git used to it. She didn' seem to like much about us down here."

"Perhaps she didn't stay long enough," Julia said. "Mrs. Wimbush, I believe I will walk to the post office and mail a letter that I wrote this morning. My parents would probably like to know that I arrived safely."

"Yes'm, well the barber shop is only open on Sa'urdays, so the Hawkinses thought it would be better if the boxes was at their store. Jimmy, he gits the mail sack ever day, so you kin jes take the letter to him. He'll put it on the next train for ya'. Mis' Alston used to be the postmistress but she's s'crippled up with authoritus n'al she can't do it no more. She lives next door to the Hawkinses. She can't git out n'about but she knows everthing that goes on in Chalk Creek."

"I'd like to meet her someday," Julia said. "I'll be back soon."

Julia recalled the words in her letter as she walked into town.

> *Dear Mama and Papa,*
>
> *I have arrived safely in Chalk Creek and I am staying in the home of a family named Wimbush. There are two children, a boy 11 and a girl 9.*
>
> *Mrs. Wimbush is reserved or shy perhaps, but kind. She is anxious for her children to get "schoolin'", even if it means boarding the school marm! At first she seemed a bit wary of me, but now I think she is becoming more friendly.*
>
> *The teacher whom I am replacing left town without telling anyone she was going. Her clothes are still in the bureau in my room. I think it is quite odd. She was from Pennsylvania.*

My salary will be thirty dollars a month. I am so proud to be earning my own money. I feel useful and needed. I do miss you very much and I pray that Judson is better.

Kisses to each of you,

Julia

P.S. Next letter I will tell you about the Budds and some of the other people I have met.

Write to me:

C/O General Delivery

Chalk Creek, Georgia

Purposefully, Julia left out a description of her living conditions. She did not want Papa to worry or to decide to come take her back home.

Hawkins' store was almost dark inside. A kerosene lamp on the counter cast a circle of light and a small red glow could be seen from the potbellied stove in the back of the one room building. Julia could see that a few canned goods, coffee, sugar, thread, head cheese and several patent medicines were available. She could smell fresh mullet, and a sign on the counter announced to fishermen:

Red Wigglers---out back.

It was a far cry from the J. M. Sutherland Co., where a man could purchase anything from a collar for his mule to a coffin for his wife.

The only other person in the store was a man. He turned, surveyed her for a moment as she closed the door and said, "Mrs. Hawkins has gone to gather me some fresh eggs. She should be back soon."

He was of average height, slightly stooped, with granite-colored hair and mustache. Except for the fact that he had no beard, he reminded Julia of the bust of Brahms that sat on the side of the piano at home.

"You must be the new teacher I understand's come to Chalk Creek. I am Dr. Samuel Weismann. Glad to have you here. How long do you figure you will last?"

"I plan to stay, Dr. Weismann." Julia smiled. "I'm Julia Sutherland. How do you do?"

"Oh, a girl with spunk?" Dr. Weismann smiled. "Well, Chalk Creek is not the most desirable place. I wish you luck."

Julia thought that she just might need that luck in Chalk Creek.

"Do you have children or grandchildren who would be in my classes, Dr. Weismann?"

"No, my son's in the army. Stationed in the Philippines now, thank goodness."

"I'm sure you are grateful he is not in France, or somewhere there is influenza. Has Chalk Creek suffered much from it?"

"I figure God's already plagued this poor pocket of humanity enough---surely He wouldn't visit us with influenza, too. I do not see patients anymore, but I haven't heard of any cases here."

At that moment Sarah Hawkins came in with a basket of eggs. She nodded at Julia but did not smile or speak.

"May I leave this letter to be mailed, Mrs. Hawkins? It was nice to have met you Dr. Weismann. I hope we can talk again sometime."

He bowed, "We shall. Soon."

As she made her way back up the rutted hill, Julia wondered about this obviously intelligent, cultured man. Why had he come to live in this backwoods part of Georgia? He did not sound like a Southerner. Perhaps, she thought, it was best not to ask about his past. Perhaps it was that past that led him here in the first place.

Rose was sweeping the porch when Julia came into the yard. She looked up and smiled broadly, "You got company, Mis' Sutherlan'."

"Oh, me?"

"Yes'm. Bitty Budd's inside. He brung his checker board."

The checker board was arranged on the small table under the window, the chairs ready. Bitty Budd stood, smiled at her and extended a closed fist. "I brung ya' sumpin', Mis' Sutherlan'."

Opening his fist into Julia's hand, he dropped a dozen or more shelled peanuts. Loose tobacco was mixed among them. "I was thinkin' you might be hongry."

His overalls were clean. He had shaved and his dark hair, parted in the middle, was slicked down on both sides of his head. "Would you like to play a little checkers?"

Julia didn't want to do this. Bitty Budd was hardly the 'immaculate man on a roan horse' that Mama had met when she arrived in Conway. On the other hand, he was Rose's cousin and she wanted to be polite."

"I'll try, Bitty Budd," she said. "But I have not played in a long time."

She had not expected his skill. After three games in which she was badly beaten, she said, "Bitty Budd, you are a shark!"

"Don't quit now," Bitty Budd said, "I'll let you win next game. You're gettin' better."

Rose came in from the kitchen. "Would you like to stay for supper, Bitty Budd?" she asked.

"Well, thank ya', Rose, I don't rightly mind if I do."

It had rained and turned bitterly cold while they played checkers. Rose's meal of hot cornbread, turnip greens and pot 'likker' seemed perfect for such a night.

During supper Clarence and Bitty Budd talked about the work at the mine. Bitty Budd said, "Seems like the war is makin' it harder n' harder to git supplies, and the railroad ain't runnin' reg'lar like it used to."

Clarence nodded his head, "I th-think you're right, Bitty Budd. And I heard that," during a long pause he struggled for the name, "J-Jim Davis and two of them other pickers and shovelers has quit to join the army. Labor's gettin' sc-sc-scarce."

"Well," Bitty Budd smiled, "I reckon the rest of us 'ul jus' have to work harder." He lifted a finely whittled toothpick from his bib pocket and placed it between his teeth. "Good supper, Rose. Thank ya'."

Clarence stood and said, "I think maybe I'm gonna go c-c-coon huntin' tonight, I'll take D-Donny. You wanna go Bitty Budd?"

"Thank ya', I don' think so. I b'leve I'll jus' stay here a while and talk to the teacher."

Moving into the front room, he chose one of the rockers by the fire and motioned for Julia to join him. She would rather have finished the book she was reading, but she could not disappoint this sweet and gentle man.

In answer to his questions, she told him about her family and a few of Papa's choice stories, mimicking the characters as Papa could. Bitty Budd's favorite was the one about an old maid.

"One time, Bitty Budd, an old maid was kneeling and praying under an apple tree. Her fervent pleas, begging, 'Dear Lord, please send me a husband', had waked an owl hidden in the branches above. The owl began calling, 'Whoo--who-whot-who.' The old maid, frightened beyond her senses, fell on her face, then righted herself and cried aloud, 'Oh, Lord, it doesn't matter Who, 'most anybody will do!'"

Bitty Budd laughed, slapped his knee, then reached over and slapped Julia's knee exclaiming, "Mis' Sutherlan', you jes won't do! Tell it again."

Julia shifted in her chair and began rocking. "Oh, Bitty Budd, once is enough."

Like a child, Bitty Budd seemed completely unaware of the impropriety of touching her knee.

"Let me tell you about owls, Mis' Sutherlan'. If owls didn't have feathers on they feet, they cud'n swoop down on they prey so silently. They fly quietly, quietly, and then they jus' swoops down," he demonstrated with his right hand, "and catches that lil' ol mouse and silently flies off."

"That's interesting, Bitty Budd."

"It are thet, Cud'n Dick," was his unusual reply.

He reached into his pants pocket and brought out a pocket knife and several kitchen matches. Julia noticed that the blade of his knife was worn thin. She watched as he dexterously whittled the matches to a sharp point without breaking them.

"I like to keep two spars all the time," he explained, and added the new ones to his cache in the bib pocket and the other, almost like a labret, between his lips.

Trying to think of something to talk about, Julia asked, "Bitty Budd, tell me about your job at the mine. I have never seen a mine. What does it look like?"

"Well, Mis' Sutherland, it's kinda like a great big deep gully," he lifted his right arm as high as it would go, "with dirt on the top and both sides. 'Bout mid-way down the sides you can see this white clay. Sometimes when I'm standin' down at the bottom of a pit it looks to me like," using both arms he made a large circle, "I'm surrounded by a giant white pillow, and in some places," he pointed with his finger, "there's a black hole in one side where the train track goes."

He took a deep breath. "You might say I do a lots of jobs. I started off as a water boy for the diggers and shovelers. I carried a ten-quart bucket of water and a dipper all over the mine." He smiled and seemed proud of this accomplishment.

"Anyway, you see, the dirt on top of the clay--- they calls it overburden---has to be got off. We uses mules, pulleys and scrapers to do this and picks and shovels to mine the clay." Moving his arms, hands and fingers to show Julia exactly how all this industry was done, Bitty Budd continued. "Some days I'm a picker and loader, and some days I work the mules, and some days I stay in the plant where the flotation troughs are."

"It sounds like hard work. Do Big Budd and your father work with you?"

"Well, not exactly. After it's cleaned and crushed the clay's wheelbarr'd to the boxcars. Pa is in charge of level'n it and coverin' it with brown paper to keep cinders from the train engine from blowin' in it. It has to be kep' clean. It goes from here to Savannah and then all over the world. Ain't that excitin', Mis' Sutherlan'?"

"I didn't even know all this treasure was in Georgia."

"Well, it are thet, Cud'n Dick. Now Big Budd, he is sorta fo'man. A long time ago he slipped on some loose gravel while he was shoveling overburden and fell into the pit. He was lucky he didn't git kilt. Most places the mine's forty to sixty feet deep, sometimes more. The mine folks' been real good to 'im."

Rose had finished the ironing she had been doing and joined them.

Julia rose, "Bitty Budd, I think I shall go to bed now, thank you for the checkers lesson."

"It shor' was nice, Mis' Sutherlan'." Bitty Budd ducked his head, then looked up and said, "Well-uh, you reckon I could call you Mis' Julya?"

Julia hesitated. She did not want to encourage him nor hurt his feelings. She smiled and said, "I suppose so, Bitty Budd. Good night."

Chapter 6--Clarence's People

Today being the first Sunday of the month there was no church.

By afternoon the day was sunny and much warmer. Julia sat in her room trying to read, but recurring thoughts of Miss Potter interfered with her concentration. It was difficult to understand how someone as neat and methodical as Miss Potter had been in the arrangement of her clothes, could be so thoughtless, reckless even, in her behavior. She was obviously a woman of some breeding, and she had the advantages of intelligence and education. She might have been unhappy here, uncomfortable perhaps, but it seemed unnecessarily rude to have treated Rose and Clarence in such a thoughtless manner.

Intrigued by the inconsistencies in this person she had never met, Julia pondered why she had suddenly left, leaving everything she owned behind. Was it the persuasion of a lover? What other reasons might have caused her to act as she did?

The repeated blaring of an automobile horn, over and over and over again, crashed into the quiet afternoon and Julia wondered who on earth would use a horn in that way. Rose had said that Mr. Northrup, Dr. Weismann and the Hawkins owned the only automobiles in Chalk Creek. Mr. Marshall lived over in Adcock.

Julia heard Clarence open the front door. Rose came out of the kitchen drying her hands. "Oh, Lord, no!" she grumbled.

Julia could hear a man calling, "Come here, Clarence, I want to show you what we just bought."

Rose muttered something not distinguishable as she went to the door. She paused at Julia's doorway and said, "Mis' Sutherlan', it's Clarence's people."

From inside Julia caught snatches of their conversation.

"It's a 1917 Dodge Brothers Four, Clarence, with a 4-cylinder engine. Straight out of De-troit. See this speedometer--it'll go sixty mile an hour--and there's even a light on this dash panel."

She heard the man mention a figure, she couldn't be sure, eight hundred and something.

An older woman's voice said, "Honey, don't touch the paint, fingerprints show up on black, you know. Rose, what's her name?"

"It's still Sari, Mrs. Wimbush. And that's still Donny. Yawl wanna' come in?"

Julia couldn't resist a peep out the front window. A shiny black roadster was parked in the yard, with black leather seats and top, wide running boards, and what appeared to be celluloid strips in the rear, probably to aid in visibility, but offering some protection from dust and rain.

The man with Clarence was short, rotund, with large eyes and almost bald. He was dressed in a neat business suit and held a black bowler hat in one hand.

The lady seemed to be a solid blob of russet from head to toe. She, too, was plump. Her large hat of rust felt was encircled with reddish feathers. Her thin hair showed evidence of roux and her skin was pinky-red. As though they had sprouted fur, her thick jowls melded into the reddish-brown beaver neckpiece on her rust colored coat. Julia could not see them, but she had no doubt that Mrs. Wimbush's shoes were reddish brown.

"I don't guess so this time, Rose," Mrs. Wimbush said. "Claud just wanted Clarence to see the new automobile and it was a nice afternoon. Come on, Claud, let's go."

Clarence said, "G-G-G-Good-bye, Mother."

Claud dutifully climbed back into the new possession and they disappeared as quickly as they had arrived. Julia retreated to her room wondering at the rudeness of this woman.

Clarence came back into the house and said only, "I'm going squirrel huntin."

Later that afternoon Julia joined Rose, who was sitting on the back porch in the sunshine sewing buttons on the children's shirts. She had snuff under her bottom lip. Julia had never seen Rose dip snuff before.

Donny was filling the wood box by the stove and Sari was milking Nanny. It was a rare opportunity for the two women to share a moment alone. They sat in silence for several minutes. Julia sensed a sadness, a heaviness about Rose.

"She don't even remember her own grandcheerun's names! She don't even try!" She bit her thread and folded the shirt. "I know I shouldn't harbor no bitterness, and I know what the Bible says about giving thanks always and being contentful in whatever condition we's in, but there are times when it almost seems like I'm savorin' my bitterness. I know I shouldn' and it don't do no good, but it just sorta feels good. It looks like they gets pleasure outta hurtin' Clarence."

There was another long pause.

Julia was afraid to say anything.

"I can't stay mad with 'em long though, 'cause fore long I realize I'm feelin' sorry for 'em. All they've got to make 'em happy is they things." She continued, "You know you don't need things, Mis' Sutherlan', to make a happy life. And we're all gonna have the same thing one a' these days. And that's six feet a dirt."

Julia nodded.

Rose leaned forward and spat over the edge of the porch.

"Clarence is a good man, Mis' Sutherlan'."

Julia was surprised by Rose's openness. She seemed eager to talk, to unburden herself, and Julia realized that Rose had no other woman or friend in whom she could confide.

"He loves his cheerun, Mis' Sutherlan'. If he hadn't been so mistreated I speck he'd a been a good carpenter. He made them yokes for the cheerun to tote the water. Or maybe even a painter. But his people, they never had no patience with him---never tried to help him learn to do nuthin'---they always seem to be embarrassed by him."

"Why was that, Rose?" Julia ventured less formality.

"Well, Clarence was born left-handed. His mother didn't want him to be. She didn' think that was good. Clarence told me it embarrassed her. It was a disgrace, so she strapped that arm to his body so he'd have to use the right one. He tol' me when he started to school he was shy, he stuttered and he was not a good student. After school he would slip off the straps and play ball with his brothers and the other boys. He had a lots of friends, but he never did finish his schoolin'."

Julia thought of the expensive automobile and recalled that Wimbush was a prominent name in Macon.

"Isn't there a public park in Macon named Wimbush Park, Rose?"

"Yes'm, Clarence said his uncle gave that land to the city. Clarence has one brother that made a doctor. He's way up yonder in Boston, and another brother, he's a lawya in Atlanta. I never met neither of them. And then Claud, thet took over his Papa's store. He brings his Mama down here about one'st ever year."

Julia shook her head. Only once a year?

Rose folded another shirt and picked up a pair of socks to darn. "After his Papa died, when Clarence was a young man, he come on to Chalk Creek to work in the mine. I think he really wanted to get away from his Ma. The Clay Company used him in the office for awhile 'cause he couldn't do no heavy work and he bought this place. The mine people was real good to him."

She changed her darning egg from one sock to the other. "I tol 'im one time I thought he'd been mistreated by his family. You know what he said Mis' Sutherlan'?"

Julia shook her head, "No, what, Rose?"

"He said, 'Well, maybe so, Rose, but if they hadn', then I wudna' come here, and then I wudna' met you. So I'm glad they did.' He's a sweet good man, Mis' Sutherlan'."

Rose finished the socks and seemed to Julia to be in better spirits. "First time we met, Clarence tol' me I was the pruttiest girl he'd ever talked to. He jus' kep'on astin' me to marry 'im---over an' over. I s'pose I thought I could hep' 'im."

That night Julia wrote in the Journal she had begun keeping.

> Rose seems to be a good, honest woman. She and Clarence speak the truth as they see it. There is no guile, no expediency. From that spark of the Divine within her, Rose tries to do what is right and leaves the results to God.

In marrying Rose had Clarence been trying to hurt his mother? Could she ever do the same to Mama?

Chapter 7--Atherton School

The sun had not yet cleared the tallest trees, and in the deep shade on the banks of the road leading to the school, brown stubby weeds and the tops of little pines were white with frost. Ice crystals edged the mud puddles and damp ruts. Julia tried to pick her way on the higher ridges of the driest mounds.

"C'mon, Mis' Sutherlan'," Donny laughed, "a little dirt ain't gonna hurtcha'. We gotta build the fire fo' the others git there."

Julia thought he must be cold. His jacket looked very thin.

"Go ahead, Donny, we're coming," Julia called.

Sari was carefully trying to step where Julia had stepped and was swinging a lard pail in one hand. "Ma put some school-bell biscuits for you with our lunch, Miss Sutherland."

"That was thoughtful, Sari. What are school-bell biscuits?"

"Well, you takes a nice, fat biscuit and you punches a hole in the top with your thumb, and you pours in molasses. Then you takes it to school for when the dinner bell rings."

"I can hardly wait to taste it."

Julia felt this might be a good chance to question Sari about Miss Potter. She wondered if Sari knew anything that Rose had not remembered. "Tell me, Sari, when was the last day that Miss Potter taught?"

"I think---I think it was the Monday before Halloween."

"Did she finish that day at school?"

"Yes'm. Most of the time we'd walk home together, but that day she said she wanted to stay and put some arithmetic problems on the blackboard. Me and Donny had extra chores that week so we come on home."

Sari was chattering on, enjoying the attention. "When she hadn't come home by supper time, Pa and Lil' Budd, they went over to the school house a-looking fo'er."

"And, of course, they didn't find her."

"No'm, they didn' find nuthin'---'cept a letter in the desk drawer from her boyfriend."

"I don't understand," Julia said. "How could someone just disappear from Chalk Creek?"

"Well, Pa and Lil' Budd read the letter, and they said it sounded like Miss Potter and this man was gonna' git married and then they had a fallin' out, and that's when Miss Potter come to Chalk Creek." Sari shrugged her shoulders, "I guess he just come and got her."

"And your Mother said she had no family?"

"No'm, she didn't have no family. She tol' us when she come in September that her Ma and Pa was dead."

Sari had been watching Julia's feet all the while she answered questions. "Mis' Sutherlan', them sure is pretty shoes you a-wearin'. I wisht I had some like 'em."

Julia's curiosity had not been satisfied, but obviously Sari wanted to think of something else.

"Well Sari, when you grow a little more I'll give them to you."

Julia noticed a narrow driveway on the right leading to a house set back from the road in a clump of trees. "Whose house is that, Sari?"

"The Simmones lives there. Billy and Raymond and Mary Louise Simmons. They'll be comin' long soon."

They walked in silence for several minutes. Then Sari asked, "You see where Donny is way up there? And them big pines beyond him?"

"Yes."

"Well, that's where the school house is at---it's right in amongst them pines."

Sari sounded happy and excited, but Julia felt a sudden tightness in her chest and her lips were dry. The confidence she possessed when she left Conway seemed, like Miss Potter, to have mysteriously disappeared.

As they drew closer, Julia could see that many years ago Atherton School had been given a coat of white paint. It badly needed another one.

Donny was waiting for them on the little front porch. One of the hounds had followed him and was already sleeping by the door, as though he were accustomed to waiting. A covered well stood in front, and two privies out back. A small woodpile was stacked against the side of the frame building.

The single classroom had windows on each side, a large blackboard behind the oak teacher's desk, and a stove in front of it with the pipe squarely in the line of vision. The two rows of children's desks were graduated in size with the smaller ones in the front. The room was cold and musty.

"Donny, let's try to get a fire started. Be careful, that flue looks very rickety."

"Yes'm, it does come loose lots of times."

On a stool near the teacher's desk was a water bucket and tin dipper. "Sari, do you think you could fill the water bucket?"

"Yes'm."

Julia took a quick appraisal of her desk drawers. She found several pencils, a speller, a few notebooks, a 1913 clothbound edition by the Macmillan Co. of The House of the Seven Gables and a similar one of Cooper's Last of the Mohicans. On the inside cover in a handwriting she had seen before was the name *K. Potter 1913   25 cents.*

If all else fails, Julia said to herself, I can read to them.

Julia stood at the open door to greet each child as he entered. Some came eagerly, obviously excited; a few looked apprehensive; some looked bored; and one large boy, at least sixteen, seemed almost belligerent. For a long time he had stood leaning against a tree outside. He was the last to enter and slumped into the nearest desk. It was too small for him and his legs extended into the aisles on either side.

There were several empty desks, but even so a brother and sister were sharing a desk and two pretty, little blond girls were squirming to divide a seat near the front.

Promptly at 8:30, Julia closed the door. As she moved toward the front of the room, she counted fifteen children of different ages and various sizes. A few had brought their spellers and composition books.

"Good morning, class." She hoped her voice did not reflect the uncertainty she felt. "My name is Julia Sutherland and I am your new teacher. I want to learn your names as quickly as possible. So before we begin our lessons, would you please stand and tell me your name and age? We'll begin on the left side of the room."

A shy looking boy with his hands jammed into his pants pockets and his chin tucked into his shirt collar rose and, without looking at her, said quickly, "I'm nine years old and my name's Adam Lee Pendley."

"Thank you , Adam, next."

This was a thin little girl with long, stringy dark hair. "I'm Emmy Lou Bankston. I'm ten, and we're glad you come, Miss Sutherland."

"Thank you, Emmy Lou."

One after another-- Hallie Maude Hardy, Melvin Wilcox, Azalee Settle, Wallace King Newman, Jesse King Newman, Billy and Mary Louise Simmons, Donny Wimbush, and Sari Wimbush stood and gave their names. Next in line was a very overweight girl, who struggled to free herself from the desk.

"My name's Tabitha Welborn and I'm seventeen."

Julia remembered Mama's telling her that Tabitha in Greek meant gazelle. The name did not seem to suit this clumsy, awkward young girl.

The large boy was next. He did not stand. With his bottom jaw protruding bulldog fashion, he said loudly, "My name's Ben Hill Madden." He emphasized the first syllable of his last name. Mad, Julia thought. One name it would not be hard to remember.

"My Pa said he'd whup me with his razor strop if I didn't come here today." Julia heard him mutter. "That's the only reason I'm here."

As she walked down the aisle nearer his desk, Ben Hill leaned back, lifted a leg, and held it up blocking her way. Julia stopped and stared at him waiting for him to move it. He stared back and did not move. Neither of them blinked. After what seemed to be an interminable silence, she asked, "Ben Hill, as the oldest boy, would you be responsible for the stove each morning?"

He shifted in his seat, scratched the back of his neck as though he were trying to rid himself of something uncomfortable, glanced quickly sideways at the younger boys. "I reckon," he shrugged

"Thank you, Ben Hill, I'll depend on you." Julia returned to her desk. Her knees were trembling. This boy was larger than she was.

The next child to speak was a lovely girl of about eleven, with Parian-like complexion, wispy blond hair and the clearest blue eyes Julia had ever seen. She did not rise and she did not speak. She looked up at Julia and smiled, an unhurried smile.

From the desk in front of her, a boy's hand shot up.

"Yes?" Julia asked.

The plump boy rose quickly. A shock of red hair bounced on his forehead as he marched to the front. He leaned over the teacher's desk and whispered loudly, "Mis' Sutherlan', she ain't all thar---you don't need to ast her no questions---she ain't all thar."

"And what's your name?" Julia asked the boy.

He straightened, "Raymond Simmons." He smiled a broad smile, pointed to the still smiling girl and added, "She's Wissie, Wissie Cochrane."

So Julia met her students and found them intriguing. Their needs and abilities were yet to be discovered. She liked them and felt that she wanted to help them if she could, but without many books or tablets this first day would be difficult.

"Class, let's begin this morning by having a geography lesson. Can any one tell me what city is the capital of Georgia?"

Azalee Settle's hand shot up.

"Yes, Azalee."

"Is it At-lanta?"

"That's right." Julia said. "Very good, Azalee. That's where our governor stays and Georgia laws are made."

After several more geography questions, Julia moved into a short history lesson. Then she put a list of spelling words on the blackboard and some arithmetic problems. While the older students worked on these, she helped the younger ones with basic reading. Several times during the day Julia made suggestions about using proper grammar. She thought it was futile, but she would keep trying.

After the dinner recess she spent the afternoon reading to the class from the <u>Last of the Mohicans</u>. By the end of the third chapter, Julia noticed Ben Hill leaning forward in his desk and listening intently to every word.

At the end of the day, Julia announced to the class that their only assignment would be to bring in for tomorrow a short essay, poem or story about their favorite gift or their most exciting experience.

"It need not be long, and we will have a good time sharing together." Julia felt that these papers would tell her a great deal about her students' abilities and their needs. "Please bring any school books you have at home and as you leave, fold your seats up. This will make it easier for me to sweep. See you tomorrow."

Wissie lingered and got the broom from the back corner. "I kin do it," she offered. She swept methodically. She seemed to be in no hurry to leave like most of the children were.

"Thank you, Wissie. You did that very well."

Julia was ready to lock the door when she heard a car outside. It was the superintendent of schools, Gilbert Dudley Marshall. Had he come to check on her?

"How did things go today, Miss Sutherland?" he asked.

"I think all right. We had fifteen children here, but very few books. I have found only two or three in the room."

"Yes, that is a problem."

"I noticed also that the coal box is almost empty, Julia added. "Where do we get more?"

"The school board members decide when to get more coal."

"Could you inform them that it is time?"

He did not answer her question. "Miss Sutherland, I trust that you are keeping accurate records. I believe in keeping full and complete records. Attendance records, behavior records---I believe in documentation."

As he was speaking his blue eyes darted sideways, back and forth, as though he did not want to look her in the eye. Julia wondered why he seemed so nervous.

"Miss Sutherland, I will drive Wissie home. It's late for her to walk."

It's late for me to walk, too, she thought, but did not say so. Wissie had begun shaking her head and saying, "I will walk. I will walk."

"Nonsense, Wissie, get in my car," Mr. Marshall commanded. "See you again soon Miss Sutherland. If there is anything, anything at all, that I can do to be of help, please let me know."

"Thank you, Mr. Marshall. We do need more coal and books." As Julia cleaned the blackboard, she watched them leave. She wondered about Wissie. Why would she want to linger at school, to walk instead of ride?

Chapter 8--
The Invitation and
Letters from Home

"Make haste, Donny, and git some more wood in this wood box before dark."

Rose had already started cooking supper when Julia walked through the back door and into the kitchen. "You want a cup a' coffee, Mis' Sutherlan'?" The grey enamel coffee pot stayed on the wood stove all the time. "How was your first day?"

The coffee was warm and strong, and coupled with the warmth of the kitchen and Rose's interest in her day, made it easy for Julia to unburden her concerns. "Rose, the children don't seem to have many books, there were almost no school supplies in the school house, and the coal box is almost empty."

Rose just nodded.

Julia continued, "One of the girls, Wissie Cochrane, is pretty and sweet, but seems to be slightly retarded. She did not want to go home."

"Yes'm. Miss Potter worried about her, too." Rose had fixed herself a cup of coffee and joined Julia at the table.

"Oh, Mis' Sutherlan', I almost forgot. Mr. Northrup's man Ralph drove over here this morning and he said Mr. and Mrs. Northrup want you to come for supper---he called it dinner---on Friday night. He said he would come for you at six o'clock."

"That's nice. Should I go, Rose?"

"I reckon so. They don't go to church, but I don't recon he's no infidel." She blew on her coffee and took a cautious sip. "They got the nicest house in Chalk Creek, but folks say he's 'bout the stingiest man that ever lived. He won't give nuthin' to nobody and he won't ever throw nuthin' away. Back of his house he's got eleven little sheds. He fills up one and he builds another, he fills that one up and he builds another." Julia smiled. "Then when he walks to town he picks up sticks and ties them in little bundles with string he carries in his pocket. I 'spose he uses them for fire wood." She put the cup down and continued, "Talk is that when he sets down to play cards, even with another couple, he slips his pants down to his knees so he won't slick 'em and they'll last longer. I hope you gits enough to eat."

Julia laughed, "He does seem eccentric. What is his wife like?"

"Well, I don't know Mis' Effie, I hardly ever see her. She ain't very friendly to folks in Chalk Creek."

"Perhaps I can tell him about some of the things we need at the school. Mr. Marshall did not seem to be very interested. Thank you for the coffee, Rose."

By the end of the week, Atherton School had three more pupils: Lou Etta Mobley and the Dunn twins, Leavis and Reavis. The Dunn twins at fourteen looked so much alike Julia decided she would have to call both names when she wanted an answer from either of them. Most of the girls had double first names. Some of them used the first name and some the middle name. When Julia asked Lou Etta would she prefer to be called Lou or Etta her reply had been, "Hit ain't neither. Hit's both, Lou-Etta-Mobley."

"All right, Lou Etta, that's what it shall be."

In spite of being short and a little overweight, Lou Etta was a rather pretty girl of fifteen. Her reddish-brown hair was naturally curly. She wore it gathered at each side behind her ears and held with red yarn. Mama would have said her large brown eyes looked like 'bull's eyes in a bowl of clabber'. Her smile revealed a gap on the left side where two teeth were missing. She seemed happy to be at school. Julia noticed that Ben Hill watched Lou Etta closely when she recited or worked a problem at the blackboard.

She wore a strong smelling little cloth bag of asafetida tied to a string around her neck. Most all of the girls did and Julia suspected that the boys may have had theirs pinned on their union suits. Perhaps it did no more good than a rabbit's foot in the pocket, but Dr. Weismann had said there had been no cases of the influenza in Chalk Creek. Wearing the asafetida bag was such a common practice, not just in Chalk Creek, that Julia wondered why anyone anywhere ever got sick.

But Wissie had not come back since the first day of school and Julia was afraid that she might be ill.

On Friday afternoon when Julia arrived at home, Rose was sweeping the yard with an elderberry broom. She was wearing a pair of Clarence's shoes. Julia had not noticed before how large Rose's feet were. The shoes fit her perfectly. Rose smiled and said, "Bitty Bud come by and brought you a letter. He said they working night and day at the mine, they so short a' help, so he can't come over tonight. I told 'em you were goin' to the Northrups anyhow. The letter's on your bed."

"Thank you, Rose."

Julia recognized Papa's strong Spenserian writing style. She was surprised and happy to receive a letter this soon. On Sutherland Company stationary she read:

Jan. 8, 1918

My dear Julia,

You have been away for less than a week, but already we miss you. Judson seems to be slightly better, however, Dr.Minter continues to come each day. He says there are no fewer cases of influenza in the county and that many people are having relapses.

I am enclosing a letter that came to you from France. We have not heard from George since his note written before Thanksgiving.

It seems from the newspapers that the British and French are looking towards America more and more for the help they need. Since the Revolution, the Russians will certainly not be much of a threat to the Hun.

We trust you are contented in your new situation.

Your loving father,

W. A. Sutherland

There was no mention of Mama.

She opened the smaller, almost square envelope to find a thick grey card edged in blue. Julia was impressed by the quality of the card. Centered at the top of the card were two crossed rifles embossed in gold. The script engraving read:

Christmas Greetings
and
Best Wishes for a Happy New Year

Stephen McCauley Whitfield
Lieutenant of Infantry
United States Army

At the bottom, written by hand, was the date December 1917. There was nothing on the back. Inside she found a small folded piece of paper, almost as thin as tissue paper. It read:

> *Dear Miss Sutherland,*
>
> *I hope that you remember me. We met at Laura Cheek's party in Macon last June. I could never forget how beautiful I thought you were and you have been on my mind for all these months. Events in my life have kept me on-the-go, but I have wanted to write to you. You were with Robert Gambell and I am gambling and hoping that you are not in love with him.*

Julia felt her cheeks growing warm. She did remember Stephen. She remembered that he had come over to the group where she was standing and asked her to dance. He was very polite and an excellent dancer. She read on.

> *When I met you, I had recently returned home from serving on the Mexican Border (1916-17) with the Macon Volunteers. I am now a member of the 42<u>nd</u> Rainbow Division, so called because we have units drawn from 36 states. In August we were assigned to Camp Mills, N. Y., and in October I was one of almost 11,000 men who sailed on the <u>Leviathan</u>, a German ship interned*

while in N.Y. harbor. We landed at Brest, France and moved into a training area in early November.

The Germans now have roughly 3,000,000 men in uniform and the potential for raising another 30 divisions. The best the Allies can muster at this time, counting 12 Belgian, 4 American and 2 Portuguese divisions is [CENSORED]

Of course the bulk of soldiers are French and British. Allied morale is at a low ebb. The rumor is that Petain believes the war is lost. I am running out of paper. It is very scarce. May I write to you again?

Kindest regards,
Stephen M. Whitfield

Julia sat on her bed and thought about the letter. A smile played at the corners of her mouth. Her heart was beating much faster than usual. She was excited, thrilled even, to have heard from this young officer.

Chapter 9--The Northrups

P romptly at six that night, Ralph arrived for Julia. As they turned into the Northrups' driveway, she remembered Little Budd's words, "You can't see his house from the road. It's up aways behind them trees."

Rounding a curve in the sandy driveway, a three-story red brick Victorian house came into view. Turrets flanked each end of the house as though guarding it against intruders, and upper and lower porches with elaborate white fretwork spanned the distance between them. It reminded Julia more of a fortress than a home.

Aquila Northrup opened the heavy mahogany door and introduced the small, fluttery woman at his side as his wife, Effie. She led the way into the living room, taking small steps and bobbing her head like a dove. Mr. Northrup hung Julia's coat on a large golden oak hat rack in the front hall. A telephone was on the wall nearby.

Mrs. Northrup pointed Julia toward a Victorian loveseat covered in shiny black horsehair. A matching pair of straight-backed chairs, equally uncomfortable looking, stood on either side. Across the room an upright piano held at least a dozen framed pictures of family members. A black hymnal leaned against the music rack. In the middle of the room, a square oak table stood on a dark patterned rug. Playing cards and dominoes waited, ready for use. Glass-enclosed book cases filled with leather bound volumes flanked each side of the fireplace.

Oddly, in the place of honor, in the center of the fireplace mantel, was an opened bottle of Coca-Cola about three-quarters full. The dusty outside of the bottle indicated that it had not been touched for a very long time. Julia wondered why in the world it was there.

On an oval marble-topped table next to the sofa, three stuffed humming birds rested on a branch incased in a clear glass dome. Their deadness seemed to Julia to symbolize the entire room. It suited Aquila Northrup she thought, as he joined them.

"Well, Miss Sutherland, I am curious about your first week of school. What do you think of Atherton School?"

Mr. Northrup's bushy brown and gray eyebrows wore a permanent crease between them. He didn't smile and in the dim, flickering light from the gas jets of the chandelier overhead, his steel-rimmed glasses created two black shadows on his face. Effie laughed nervously.

"It is a very nice school, Mr. Northrup," Julia said. "I have been pleased with the number of students attending. Of course they don't all come every day, but for the most part they seem eager to learn."

She paused and chose her words carefully. "We do seem to have a serious problem with a lack of books and supplies, especially for the older, more advanced students. We also need more coal for the stove. The children seem too poor to pay for their books. Do you think that you and Mrs. Northrup would like to buy some books for the school?"

The crease between Mr. Northrup's eyebrows seemed to deepen. "Miss Sutherland, as you are aware, Atherton School is a free school, or as some refer to them, a 'pauper school'. The largest single item in the school budget is the teacher's salary. It is expensive, and many people would say unnecessary, to educate 'all of the children of all of the people'."

Julia's eyes widened in disbelief. She found it incredible that this was the chairman of the school board speaking.

He continued, "The Good Book expresses my feelings exactly, Miss Sutherland, when it speaks of the leech having two daughters, 'Give and Give'." His high, stiff collar seemed to be getting tighter as he spoke, and the gold stick pin worn high in his tie moved with each emphatic word. "I am asked quite often by someone to 'Give, Give' to some cause or eleemosynary institution. No! I believe, as the Good Book says, 'Charity begins at home'."

Julia knew those last words were not in the Bible and she wondered just how much of it he had read.

"If they want to read badly enough they, like Lincoln, can borrow a book."

Without a moment's hesitation Julia asked, "Do you have a few I may borrow tonight, Mr. Northrup? I never imagined that there would be no books at the school."

He cleared his throat and said, "I doubt if your students are ready for my books just yet, Miss Sutherland."

Julia started to protest, but with an air of finality, he pulled down on his vest, checked the gold pocket watch and said, "Shall we go in to eat now? Dr. Weismann is joining us later for cards."

During dinner Mrs. Northrup tried to speak, "Miss Sutherland, I hope you like chicken breasts, rice and -----"

"Effie, you can see Miss Sutherland likes it. She's eating it, isn't she?" Mr. Northrup said.

Julia felt sorry for her. She wondered if Mrs. Northrup ever got to finish a sentence.

Mr. Northrup spoke at length about the war. "We have absolutely no business getting involved in this conflict. It is not up to us to solve the world's problems. The French can't fight. They deserve what they get."

He did not seem to want to hear another opinion. He knew the correct answers so Julia said nothing.

Miss Effie tried to change the subject. "Miss Sutherland, what business is your father---"

"We know that, Effie, he's a farmer," Mr. Northrup said.

Julia said, "Yes, Miss Effie. He doesn't actually do the work, but he owns the land, the mules and equipment. He has many good helpers on the place, some families have been with him all of their lives, and he is very fond of them. They depend on my father and he depends on them."

"I perceive that you admire your father very highly."

"Oh, I do indeed, Mr. Northrup. If there should be a succinct description of him, of his philosophy of life, I believe it would be that verse from the Psalmist that says: 'Trust in the Lord and do good'. And," she added, "he seems to find many opportunities to do just that." She could quote the 'Good Book' as well as Mr. Northrup, she thought.

As they moved back into the parlor, striving for something encouraging to say to her hostess, Julia complimented the meal and added, "Mrs. Northrup, I think you have the daintiest hands and feet I have ever seen."

"You can't see her skinny legs, Miss Sutherland, but I can tell you that if only I could bore a hole in a cotton string, I would never have to buy her any more stockings!" He laughed at what he considered a humorous remark.

Nervous laughter was his wife's only response.

Then Effie asked timidly, "Miss Sutherland, do you know anything about your origins---your name? Miss Potter did not seem to know anything about her family, only that her grandfather had served in the Union army. She told me he was killed at Chancellorsville."

Julia thought of the silver locket with the picture of the uniformed man inside. How could Katherine Potter have left such an heirloom? Mama would never part with the gold locket that had belonged to her mother. She always wore it.

"Before I was married," Miss Effie continued, "I was a Perkins, of The Perkins from Vidalia."

"I don't know much, Mrs. Northrup, but my father has always said that the Sutherlands came from northern England. The name was given to them by the Vikings, who ventured to the English shores and considered it south of their land."

Feeling that she would like to lighten the mood, Julia added, "He has also cautioned that we should not look back too far, for we may discover a horse thief somewhere."

"Well, I suppose maybe so."

Oh dear, Julia thought. Miss Effie took her seriously.

"Miss Sutherland, I would like to show you my post-card collection. Do you like post-cards?"

"Not now, Effie. I hear Dr. Weismann's car."

Julia was delighted to see the doctor, and he seemed glad to see her again as well.

Mr. Northrup announced that they would play Whist. "All games at cards are insignificant in comparison with Whist. It is believed to take its name from an old expression 'to keep silence' and it must be conducted noiselessly and with exact attention."

Both were extremely difficult for Mrs. Northrup.

Whist was similar to bridge and Julia caught on quickly. Remembering what Rose had said about Mr. Northrup lowering his pants while playing cards, at one point during the game Julia let one of her cards fall to the floor. As she picked up the card she checked the condition of Mr. Northrup's trousers, but this time could detect nothing unusual.

When it was time to leave, Dr. Weismann offered to drive Julia home.

As he opened the door for her, she said, "This looks like a very comfortable automobile, Dr. Weismann."

"It's a Hudson sedan. I bought it after the electric self-starter was invented. I had seen so many men get broken wrists from those hand cranks."

As they headed down the Northrup's drive, Julia took the opportunity to ask about Wissie. "Dr. Weismann, I want to ask you about the Cochrane family. Are you familiar with them? Particularly Wissie?"

"Well, I know who they are and where they live. Wissie seems somewhat slow, and Durrell Cochrane is about the laziest man I have ever seen. Why?"

"I am concerned about her. She was at school on Monday but has not been back. She may be sick. I think I shall go to see her."

"Well, you be careful. Durrell Cochrane is not only lazy, he is mean. He does not work at the mine and only occasionally at the sawmill. Most people think that he and his boys make whiskey somewhere on his place."

"I think it is very strange that Miss Potter would have left Chalk Creek so suddenly, without settling her rent or saying good-bye. Did you get to know her?"

"No, I didn't really. She was not very friendly and I think quite unhappy here in this poor area. I believe that she was disappointed that she could not change and improve the education level quickly. I'm afraid that will take a long time."

Julia nodded.

They pulled up in front of the Wimbush house and as he turned off the motor he added, "I don't know how she accomplished it, but I have always thought it highly unlikely that Miss Potter could leave Chalk Creek and Sarah Hawkins not notice her, either with or without her boy friend."

Julia laughed. "I do wonder how she accomplished that."

As Dr. Weismann walked her to the door he said, "My wife does not go out, Miss Sutherland. If you should walk to Hawkins Store again, come by to see us."

"I shall, thank you."

Julia thought he sounded lonely.

Chapter 10--The Cochranes

The Cochrane place was almost a mile beyond the school. There were no other houses nearby. Julia noticed a thin trail of smoke rising from somewhere in the trees that edged a small unplowed corn field in back of the dilapidated house. Wet overalls, shirts and socks were hanging on a listing fence that separated the corn stalks from the littered yard.

Julia had planned to go up to the house and knock, until she saw someone she thought must be Mrs. Cochrane leaning over a black iron wash pot out in the back. With a thick stick the woman lifted a shirt out of the steaming water and dropped it on a scrub board. Sensing someone approaching, she turned her head slightly and glanced up at Julia out of the corner of her eyes.

"Hello, Mrs. Cochrane. I am Julia Sutherland, the new teacher."

Mrs. Cochrane straightened and without smiling answered, "I figger'd you wuz. Whut kin I do fur ya?" she said without smiling.

From a small shed, where wood was not stacked but scattered on the ground, Durrell Cochrane, ax in one hand

and a piece of wood in the other, walked toward Julia. He got as far as the fence, stopped and spat a long stream of brown juice in her direction.

From the house, Wissie came down the back steps smiling, her eyes lowered. Her young breasts pushed against the dress she had outgrown long ago. She was trying to pull a thin sweater across her chest when Julia noticed several large bruises on Wissie's arms and wrists where the sweater sleeves were too short.

Throwing the piece of wood and narrowly missing Wissie's foot, Durrell Cochrane shouted, "G'wan back in tha house, girl, and git supper fixed. Teacher don' need to talk to you."

Wissie turned but could not have missed hearing her father as he continued, "She ain't got good sense and there ain't no need in her settin' in thet schoolhouse. She ain't rite bright, but she can wash n'clean n' cook n'chop wood. She don't need no schoolin'. She cain't learn nothin' no how."

"I came, Mr. Cochrane, because I was concerned about Wissie. I am glad to know that she is not sick."

"Well she ain't sick. She ain't none of yo' bizness. That other teacher kep' pokin' and pryin' around an tendin' to things thet were none of her bizness, either."

"You know, Mr. Cochrane, the Georgia Legislature passed a Compulsory Attendance Law and....."

"No gd'dam legislature's goin' to tell me what to do! This is my fam'ly and my place and I wan' you outta here!" He shouted and shook the ax in her direction. Abruptly he turned and started back to the shed.

Mrs. Cochrane had begun scrubbing the shirt. Without looking up at Julia, she whispered, "He made his boys go through fourth grade. It ain't fair. Wissie enjoyed Monday at school. I kin do her chores when he ain't lookin'. She'll be back sometimes."

As she walked home, Julia thought about Katherine Potter's unfinished letter to Claire. Could Durrell Cochrane's treatment of his daughter be the "evil" she had written of? Or was there more to this situation than Julia knew about?

Chapter 11--Chalk Creek

Later that day Julia walked into town to get Rose some bluing for her wash and to mail two letters, one to Stephen Whitfield and the other to Mama and Papa. She told them about the school and Wissie, and asked them to send her some books, especially Maeterlinck's play <u>The Blue Bird</u>. She thought this pretty fairy tale about two children's quest for happiness would be important for her students to know.

As she was leaving Hawkins' store a strange-looking man in rumpled clothes walked past her in the middle of the road. He had long hair and was followed by three large geese moving in single file. When he stopped to pick up something in the road, the geese stopped. When he began walking again they, too, began walking. He led them over to a grassy place at the edge of the road where the geese could graze. She stood and watched. After a few minutes Julia heard him talking to them.

"'Com'on, Goodness, Com'on Shirley. Com'on'." Then the group moved out of sight around the curve. Julia thought she would ask Rose about him.

While she was in town, Julia decided to accept Dr. Weismann's invitation to come for a visit. But when she knocked at their door, Dr. Weismann opened it just a crack and said, "I'm sorry, Miss Sutherland, my wife is sleeping." He closed the door.

Wondering about the doctor's strange behavior,

Julia continued home and thought about her next letter to Papa. He would enjoy hearing about the strange man with the geese, and also about Aquila Northrup. She decided she would not write him about Durrell Cochrane and his threat.

When Julia reached the house, Rose was mending socks by the fire. The children were bringing water up from the spring.

Julia said, "Rose, I saw the strangest man passing Hawkins store. He had three geese that followed him. Who is he?"

Rose chuckled, "Oh, that's ol' Eppen Garrett. Most folks 'round here call him 'Pink'."

"Pink?"

"Yes'm, he's part Cherokee you know." Rose smiled. "He's m' milk brother, and a half wit you might say."

"He is your what?"

"I calls him m' milk brother, 'cause when I was born, my Ma, she didn' have no milk. I guess 'coz she was so upset and embarras'd by the way my Pa had done her."

Julia wanted to ask what had happened to her father, but didn't feel she knew Rose well enough. Perhaps someday, but not yet.

"Anyhow," Rose went on, "she'd carry me down to his ma's place three or four times a day and Mis' Garrett, she would nurse me. Eppen's three weeks older than me. He ain't got sense enough to bell a buzzard! Ma always said Eppen didn' have no sense 'cause I got all the stren'th outta his Ma's milk. You reckon that could be so Mis' Sutherland?"

Julia said, "I expect you were going to be smart anyway, Rose. Smart and energetic."

Rose blushed, and continued, "Them geese, they like pets. He named 'em Shirley, Goodness and Mercy 'cause he said th' preacher says they'll follow ya' all the days of ya' life. And they do. They'll attack ya' if you bother Eppen. Some of the boys, out of meanness, used to chunk rocks at 'im. One time they threw a hornet's nest at 'im, but they soon quit 'cause them geese, they'd attack 'em. Folks say he's crazy, but maybe I jus' got all his Ma's stren'th. I feel real sorry for 'im."

"Rose, Dr. Weismann had invited me to come to see them. I thought I would tell him about Wissie so while I was in town I knocked on their door. He opened it just a crack and said his wife was sleeping. The draperies were drawn and it looked very dark inside. Is she ill?"

"Mis' Sutherlan', no one ever sees her. Folks say she is a ad-dict."

"Oh, that's tragic, Rose. I am sorry. I wonder what she is addicted to."

"I don' know'm. Like I said, no one ever sees her."

Julia wondered if this might explain why Dr. Weismann no longer practiced medicine. But why of all places would he come to Chalk Creek?

On Monday and for the next few weeks Wissie was back at school. "Pa is working at the saw mill," Wissie said, "and Ma said I should bring Traynham. He's seven and he needs to learn to read."

Although Wissie lacked the ability to make judgments, she was wonderful with the younger children. She spent recess time playing with the little ones and tried very hard to be "normal". She wanted to dust and sweep and do anything to please Julia, and to stay at school as long as she could.

On the last Friday of January, Gilbert Dudley Marshall appeared at school at the close of the day.

"Miss Sutherland," he said, "I have made arrangements to take Wissie to Macon on Monday to be tested at the Institute for Mental Retardation. She will be absent that day."

"Do you think her father will let her go, Mr. Marshall?"

"He doesn't have to know, Miss Sutherland. We should be back by the end of the school day, and if there are any questions I feel sure you can handle them. It might be helpful to know how she tests."

"Well I would hate for him to take his anger out on Wissie if he does not approve." Julia felt uneasy about this deception. She did not like the idea of being a party to anything that might bring harm to Wissie.

"I will be here for her shortly after nine." That ended the discussion.

As she walked home, Julia wondered about Mr. Marshall's wife and family. She felt he would be a difficult man to live with, but perhaps at home, she reasoned, when he is not Superintendent, he may relax and not be so edgy. She hoped so.

When she reached the house, Julia asked Rose if she had ever met Mrs. Marshall. "Yes'm. I have. She's kindly pretty, but I reckon---well I reckon you'd say she's mousy. She don' have much to say, she's jes' kindly mousy."

Julia told her about Mr. Marshall's plan to have Wissie tested.

"I guess he's tryin' to do a good job," Rose said.

"I hope so," Julia said.

Next morning, Saturday, Bitty Budd walked into the yard bringing a box to Julia. "Mis' Hawkins said it come on las' night's train. It seemed like it was too heavy for you to carry, Mis' Julya, and I was comin' this way anyway."

Rose smiled. "Stay for dinner, Bitty Budd?"

"Thanks, Rose. I b'leve I will."

The box from Papa contained arithmetic books and spellers, copies of <u>Evangeline</u>, <u>The Blue Bird</u>, <u>Moby Dick</u>,

<u>Aesop's</u> <u>Fables</u>, <u>Treasure</u> <u>Island</u>, <u>A</u> <u>Girl</u> <u>of</u> <u>the</u> <u>Limberlost</u>, with the notation on the inside cover in Mama's handwriting, 'First American book to be translated into Arabic', and the Elson Readers series I, II, III and IV. Julia thought of the bookcases that lined both sides of the wide upstairs hall, and knew that these few copies would not be missed. Also inside the box were tablets and pencils and a thick letter from Papa. Julia was delighted.

Rose came to Julia's doorway and asked, "Mis' Sutherlan', would you mind watch'n this piece of paper in the oven door for me? When it gits medium to dark brown, please put in that pan a' biscuits? I'm fixin' to go to the privy. I'll be back ter'rectly. Bitty Budd has gone with Donny to dig for grub worms. They'll go catfishin' later."

While she waited in the kitchen for the paper to turn brown, Julia read Papa's unusually long letter.

> *My dear Julia,*
>
> *Your letters sound as though you are having interesting and challenging experiences. We hope these books will be of help to you. This letter will reveal both triumphs and tragedy for us and Conway.*
>
> *First the good news: Dr. Minter says that Judson, at least for now, is out of danger. He is up some of the time and gaining strength every day.*

Thank goodness, Julia said to herself. Prayers have been answered.

We have had three letters from George. They all came in the same mail. He has been in heavy trench fighting. When he wrote at the end of December he was still all right, but spoke of extreme weariness, cold, marching for hours in mud and landscapes so fought over that they were bare of any vegetation, not a blade of grass.

He says we must not believe everything we read in the American newspapers, but it is true that the Germans have used poison gas and that the British in the third battle of [CENSORED] lost 400,000 peach trees between July and November of last year in a five mile area. We think George was using the code words 'peach trees' because he knew that the letters were censored and that we understood how devastating such a loss can be.

Do you remember that President Wilson was re-elected in 1916 on the promise of keeping America out of the war? I wish to God it could have been so. The Fawcetts, the family that lives down on the river, received word last week that their son, Roy (the best one of the bunch) was killed in December.

Julia, in your last letter, you asked us to see if Miss Janie would make a dress for the child Wissie. I'm sorry to have to tell you of another terrible tragedy. Last Tuesday night, sometime 'way in the night, I heard

Herbert outside calling me and knocking loudly on the back door. When I looked out I could see that the sky toward town was fiery red and smoke was billowing up. We got in the Ford and drove toward the fire. Julia, it was the dormitory. Mr. Calder, the new history teacher, and Miss Janie died in the fire.

"Oh, no," Julia said out loud.

Mrs. Calder got out. You remember they lived upstairs. Mr. Calder would not leave until he got all of his books out. We could see him run to the window with an arm load, throw them out, disappear, then come again with another load. Mrs. Calder was outside crying and screaming and everyone was calling to him to jump, forget the books. All of us outside were passing buckets of water, but that wooden building went up like lighter wood. Miss Janie's remains were found where her iron bed had collapsed onto the floor below. The volunteers seemed to think she died from the smoke before the fire got to her. I'm sorry to have to tell you this.

We hope your school work is going well, and that you are happy. I remain,

Your devoted father,
W. A. Sutherland

Still there was no word from Mama.

Julia sat stunned. She thought of the little book Miss Janie had left for her, and of the fact that she had expected Miss Janie to always be available whenever she was needed.

She thought of Grady Fleming, one of Papa's hands, who was so impressed with the building when it was completed that he named his first son, "Dormitory". Later, when the school added two new classrooms, he named a new baby, "Annex".

She wondered about Mrs. Funderburk, the proprietress, whom Mama often said, "sets a nice table even on short notice. With a tea bag and a piece of ham, she could serve the Queen."

Footsteps on the back porch and smoke coming from the paper in the oven door brought Julia back to reality. "Oh, Rose, I am so sorry. I was...."

Rose took charge, scattered the smoke with a towel, and the incident was mentioned no further.

Julia tried to make amends. Sitting at the kitchen table, they began peeling and coring apples for a pie. Thinking of Mama, Julia asked, "Rose, how old were you when your mother died?"

"I was fourteen, Mis' Sutherlan', so I can remember her real good. You know I ketch m'self sometimes sayin' things thet sound jes like my Ma. I always tol' m'self when I was a girl thet I wouldn' never say things like she did---she was a fusser if ever there was one---but all of a sudden, out it will come, and I wisht I hadn' a said it. At times she liked to drove me crazy! For a long time I didn't know how I felt about her. Now---after all these years---I think maybe my Ma did the best she could."

"My father's letter had sad news from Conway, but my mother is so angry with me for defying her that she won't even write to me," Julia said. "With Mama, everything has to be done her way. If it's not her way it's wrong. I sometimes think I have to *earn* her love. I guess I love her, but I really don't like her."

"I know what you mean, Mis'Sutherlan'," Rose said. We tell ourselfs we're not gonna be like 'm, but we are. I even seem to hurt m'self in the same places my Ma did---like hittin' my right elbow when I go through a door. We try to be different, but I don' guess we really are."

"And why do mothers so often seem to favor their sons?" Julia continued. "My Mother has always let her boys have or do whatever they wanted. I am <u>not</u> going to be that way if I ever have children."

Rose thought a moment and answered slowly. "I d'know, Mis' Sutherlin---maybe mothers realize they boys wont be there very long---they'll up and git 'em a girl and be gone. A daughter, you kin kinda depend on her to be there when you need her, even if she's gone and gotten married."

She arranged cut-up apples onto the pie crust. "Or maybe, they jes' know thet big men, like little men, needs a lot-ta spoilin'. My Papa---"

She was going to continue, but Donny bounded up the back steps and called, "Ma, look at my pet," interrupting her. Donny was followed by Bitty Budd and Clarence carrying cans of worms. Donny cracked open his tightly-held hands just enough to show them a small brown frog, "Bitty Budd caught 'im for me. He's m' pet. You wanna hold'im, Mis' Sutherlan'?"

"Aren't you afraid of getting warts, Donny?" Julia smiled. "Look at all those warts on him."

"He's a Southern toad, Mis' Julya," Bitty Budd said. "They not like green tree frogs thet sound lik'a cowbell and have smooth skin---no warts. They are thet, Cud'n Dick."

Rose said, "Donny, if you want to keep him for a few days get one of those jars, put some holes in the lid and put some grass and twigs inside. As soon as you finished I need more wood in thet wood box."

"Yes'm." Donny hurried to fix his pet and finish his chores.

After dinner Bitty Budd looked at Julia and asked, "Miss Julya, you wanta go walk or play some checkers?"

Donny scowled, "Aw no, Bitty Budd, you kin play checkers with the teacher any time. We got the worms, les' go fishin'. Pa smelled a bream bed in the creek yesterday and I know right where it is. We kin really catch 'em."

From the frown on his face, Julia could see the debate taking place in Bitty Budd's head. He seemed to dislike disappointing Donny, but it was evident he wanted to be with her.

117

She quickly resolved his dilemma.

"Bitty Budd, I need to spend this afternoon getting my lesson plans outlined for the coming month. Perhaps we can play checkers some other time."

Julia went to her room, but it was not lesson plans that were on her mind. She wanted to write in her journal of the interesting and unusual people she had met in Chalk Creek--Eppen, Dr. Weismann, and Wissie. Instead she wrote to Mama and Papa to express her joy at Judson's recovery. Overwhelming all her thoughts, however, was the tragedy of the sudden deaths of people she knew back home in Conway.

She wrote,

> *Dear Mama and Papa,*
>
> *I was distressed and deeply saddened by the news of the fire and the Fawcett boy. What a tragedy! Three deaths in Conway in one week! Are there any more cases of influenza? Thank goodness Judson is improving. Please kiss him for me.*
>
> *Thank you for sending the books and school supplies. They were badly needed and will be helpful.*
>
> *There are many unusual people here in Chalk Creek. Remind me to tell you about them in detail. Papa, you would enjoy meeting a man named Eppen Garrett who has three geese that follow him everywhere. He has named them Shirley, Goodness and Mercy.*

The pupil I am most concerned about is an eleven-year-old who is a very slow learner. Her name is Wissie and she is pretty but her mother and father are not helpful to her. I hope I can be.

I realize how blessed I have been to have you for my parents.

My love,

Your daughter,

Julia

She did not want to tell them what she really thought about Durrell Cochrane.

Chapter 12--February

Gilbert Dudley Marshall did not bring Wissie back to school on Monday. Julia decided that the testing must have lasted longer than anticipated and that he had taken Wissie directly home. Tuesday Wissie walked in bringing Traynham and clutching a small, blond doll. She let each of the other girls hold it briefly, then spent the day playing with it and drawing pictures at her desk.

At recess time Julia noticed that Ben Hill and Lou Etta did not join in any of the games but sat together under one of the few schoolyard trees and shared some biscuits. Tabitha Ruth also never played with the others. She just sat and watched and ate. The gregarious and energetic Dunn twins were effective in organizing games of Hide the Stick, Crack the Whip, or today's choice of Fox and Geese. They were good leaders but they were identical, and some of the children complained that it was too hard to tell whether Leavis or Reavis was the Fox.

Wissie did not want to play with the young children today. She stayed close to Julia. It was a warm day but she had on black wool stockings and kept her sweater buttoned up all the time. She was affectionate, but Julia thought she also seemed fearful, with no luster in her eyes. She kept her head down most of the time, holding her hands, as though to close in her body protectively.

"Were the questions on the tests you took very difficult, Wissie?"

Julia's only answer was a blank stare and a weak smile. Wissie cuddled the doll, stroking the blond hair and kissing it over and over on the lips. She seemed to be somewhere else, in a fantasy land of her own design.

At the end of the day she presented Julia, as a special gift, one of the pictures she had been drawing. It was surprisingly well-done and easy to decipher. In the center of the picture was a level clearing. It was surrounded by small trees and bushes and populated by two stick people. The top, bottom and sides of her drawing were very dark, as though a storm were brewing. The details of a path and rocks were quite distinct.

"This is an interesting picture, Wissie," Julia said. "You did a good job. Would you tell me about it."

Wissie shook her head. "Secret." She was rubbing her bruised wrist.

"All right. It's your secret."

Julia was cleaning the blackboard. Wissie came close to her.

"He says I pretty. He says I not stupid. He like me. He says he cares about me. Only one who does."

"Who, Wissie? Who says this to you?"

"Can't tell. Secret."

Julia thought that considering the treatment Wissie received from her father, it would be natural for her to imagine some boy being kind and attentive. A fantasy. Poor child.

"Well, Wissie, you are pretty. Everyone does like you. You are helpful to me in the classroom. You complete your chores, and you play with the younger children quite well."

Wissie smiled and her eyes lit up.

"I'll tell you a secret," Julia said. "I had an imaginary playmate once myself. My mother told me when I was a little girl that I talked out loud to someone named Sugar Puddin'. I would not tell anyone what Sugar Puddin' said to me, and I would not let anyone sit where Sugar Puddin' was sitting."

"Sugar Puddin', Sugar Puddin'," Wissie recited over and over, then laughed out loud. It was the first time Julia had ever heard her do that.

Julia had set a goal for herself of visiting the home of each of her students by the end of February. She had almost completed it. Meeting their parents and knowing their situation at home enhanced her understanding of them and the challenges they faced. She discovered that Lou Etta was an only child. Her parents, like many of the Chalk Creek inhabitants, had little formal education and they were extremely proud of their daughter. Mr. Mobley's job was to climb the fire tower three times every day to check for fires in the area. He also worked occasionally at the mine.

While Julia was in their home, Mrs. Mobley said, "You know, Mis'Sutherlan', Lou Etta loves school. She wants t'finish and be a teacher like you."

"I hope she will, Mrs Mobley. Lou Etta is a smart girl."

"If she does, she'd be the firs' one in our fam'ly."

On her visit to the Maddens, she learned that Ben Hill's grandfather had started the sawmill operation. It passed to his father and some day would belong to Ben Hill. Each spring they planted a field of sugar cane and in the fall operated a well-patronized syrup mill.

Mr. Madden explained to Julia, "We sets out our buckets of skimmin's in the field in the sunshine. If ya' leave it there awhile it'll go to workin'. You jus' have to be sure no hawgs git to it. The durn hawgs'll git drunk. It mus' be good 'cause folks around here gits in line to buy our syrup."

The days were beginning to stay light a bit longer now, and as she walked home from one of these visits Julia noticed a chattering flock of cedar waxwings that had settled in a wild cherry tree. Papa's short letter this week had mentioned that:

'the pear trees have almost finished blooming, and the Japanese magnolia in your mother's garden and the large camellia by our bedroom window are covered in blooms. The field under the pecan trees is once again alive with dancing yellow jonquils.'

His words on the paper had blurred from tears in her eyes. She would miss spring in Conway this year.

Rose was sitting on the front steps holding two jonquils when Julia walked into the yard. They were the only blossoms from a single plant under the chinaberry tree.

"Every year when these bloom I wonder who it was thet planted 'em," she said. "Was it someone young, or someone old? Was she colored or white? I wonder, an' there's no one left to ask. I wishst I knew. I'd like to thank'm 'cause they give me so much pleasure."

Julia joined her on the steps and they watched as Donny and Sari came up the path from the spring with the water pails.

"Mama," Sari said excitedly, "them lil' bluets down by tha' spring, they gonna be bloomin' soon, and we saw two robins settin' on the bank. Spring's comin'."

Donny scratched one leg with the opposite foot, "Come on, Sari, this's gettin' heavy," he said. They moved around the corner of the house.

Being alone Julia thought this might be a good time to ask Rose about her father.

"Rose, one day you started to tell me about your father."

"Yes'm, I did. It's a long, sorry story, but knowing it kinda hep's me understan' my ma. She was the younges' of twelve sisters. Each of 'em had names that rhymed. Mama's name was Selene. Then there was Willene, Francene, Eulene,

Marlene, Ailene, Paulene, Nanilene, an I forget the rest of they names."

Julia smiled.

Rose held a jonquil to her nose and took a deep breath. "Big Budd was the only boy, he was next to ma, an' his first names' David. I guess my gran'ma figur'd it'd take a David to put up with that many girls. They lived down in Bristol, 'n I don' know where none of 'em lives now."

"That was a large family," Julia said.

"Yes'm, it was. My ma was born at the beginnin' of the war with the nawth. She tol' me her pa didn't come home from the war and things was real, real hard fa' 'em. They lik to starved to death. If it had'n been fa' possum they might have."

Julia said, "Mama has told me that many women and children did starve to death after the war, especially in the mountains."

"Yes'm. Times was terrible hard. Anyhow when ma was sixteen, that woulda been 1877, a Yankee drummer come through Bristol selling buttons, piece goods an' lace. Ma said he was a good-lookin' man and he said he loved 'er, so she ran away with 'im."

Julia shook her head.

"She tol' me they traveled on the train all over Georgia. They went to Savannah, Columbus, Macon, Tifton---even into nawth Georgia. They slep' in hotels an' boardin' houses, an' Ma said she had never been s'happy."

Rose looked down at her feet, rubbed some dirt from her shoe and continued. "Then several months later she reeliz'd somethin' was different. She was in a family way. When she tol' my Pa, he seemed happy enough, but the next mornin' when she woke up he was not there.

Shaking her head, Julia said, "Oh, no."

Rose continued. "She said she waited all day in the room until the cleanin' girl come in an' tol' her he had checked out early thet mornin'. The ticket agent at the station tol' her he thought he remember'd a man thet sounded like him, with two large suitcases, buyin' a ticket to Memphis."

"That's so sad," Julia said.

Rose nodded. "Poor Ma, she didn' have no money an' no place to go. She said none of the fam'ly would have nothin' to do with her, they was so embarrassed. My Pa was not only a Yankee, he was a Republican!"

Julia smiled, and suppressed a laugh.

Rose continued. "So Ma wrote to Big Budd, her brother. He had come here to Chalk Creek to work at the saw mill an' married Lillie Ben. They tol' her they would take her in. She said she washed dishes at the hotel until she could get enough money to buy a ticket to Chalk Creek."

Julia could see on Rose's face a mixture of emotions: sadness for her Mother's desperate plight, and pride in her determination to overcome it.

"Now, Mis' Sutherlan', let me tell you about Lillie Ben. Lillie Ben was a saint walkin' on this earth. After Ma died with consumption, she raised me. Then when Lil' Budd's wife died she raised Bitty Budd." Rose pointed to the door of the house. "You see thet china door knob on the front door, Mis' Sutherlan'? Well Lillie Ben gave it to us for a weddin' present. Cos we still use the wooden latch bar on th' inside, but I thought it would look better n' an ol' string on the outside. She ordered it from Sears an' Roebuck. I sure do miss her."

Julia said, "Do you think Miss Potter did the same thing your mother did, Rose?"

Rose frowned. "Yes'm," she said nodding her head. "I cud'da tol' Mis' Potter she wasn't gonna regret runnin' off with thet boy friend but oncet---an' thet would be fa' the rest of her life."

Chapter 13--The Accident

Bright sunshine, appearing after a week of cold, rainy, damp days, gave Julia hope that the potbellied stove would not be needed today. But once inside the school room that morning, she knew that the March chill must be warmed. The coal scuttle beside her desk was empty and the split wood pile was almost exhausted.   Most of the children were already at their desks and a few were opening their books. Adam Pendley was amusing himself and his desk mate with a wadded paper ball, thumping it into the empty ink well, retrieving it, and doing it again. Emmy Lou Bankston and Azalee Settle were whispering softly, giggling and sharing secrets.

Julia glanced at the watch on her neck chain and saw that it was almost time to begin lessons. The Dunn twins had not arrived yet, and she knew Ben Hill Madden was working for his Pa this week at the saw mill. Through the window she saw the twins rounding the curve at the tree line, dawdling along, taking turns kicking a rock along the narrow road. Julia went out to the porch steps and beckoned to them to hurry along. Much to her surprise, Ben Hill came into view. He really seems to want to learn, she thought.

Wissie had not come this morning. Julia wondered if her father had been scolding her again. Then she remembered that this was Monday, wash day, and Wissie might be helping with the wash.

"Hurry up, boys," she said. They were within shouting distance now. "I need you to split some wood and bring in a scuttle of coal."

They were running now. They were on a mission.

"You git the coal, Ben Hill. Leavis and I kin handle the wood."

Julia returned to the classroom, confident that the boys could handle this chore. She opened the stove and crumpled some newspaper to put inside on the bottom. Ben Hill came in the door with his scuttle of coal. As she turned to reach for more paper from the neat stack kept on the floor near the stove, her eyes moved to the window and she saw Leavis raise the ax. At that same instant, his brother leaned over to straighten the piece of wood, and the ax came down. Blood flowed from Reavis's head and began to cover his face.

Julia screamed but no sound came. For an instant she thought she was going to faint. Drawing strength from she knew not where, she wheeled around and said, almost softly but with stern authority, "Azalee run, run fast and get Mrs. Dunn. Ben Hill, listen to me. Run, don't stop, until you find Lil' Budd. Tell him to bring his truck---and hurry!"

Julia and Azalee left the room together. When she reached the twins, Leavis was on his knees cradling Reavis like a baby in his arms. Leavis's eyes were wide, frightened, and brimming with tears. Clean paths on his cheeks showed where rivulets of tears had already flowed.

"Oh, Miss Julia", he sobbed, "I dun kilt my brother!" Blood was oozing rapidly from Reavis's head. It circled on Leavis's sleeve and was making a puddle in the dirt.

Instantly Julia tore the large sailor collar from her blouse and wound it tightly around Reavis' head. His eyes were closed but he was breathing.

"Leavis, let's try to lift him inside out of this cold. Do you think we can?"

"Oh, yes'um, we can." It seemed to relieve him to be doing something.

"I've sent Azalee to get your mama, and Ben Hill has gone for Lil' Budd and the truck." Julia thought that if riding in the truck did not kill him, being hit in the head with an ax certainly would not.

Julia had not realized how heavy a fourteen-year-old boy could be. As they reached the door, she could hear the scurrying of eleven pairs of feet returning to their desks from the windows. Once the door was opened there was not a sound.

They laid Reavis on the floor near Julia's desk. Blood was already beginning to seep through the white collar. It was at this moment that cold fear gripped Julia. This boy could die here in her arms. She looked up at the classroom of silent, frightened children and said quietly, "Would you pray with me?"

Eleven heads and Leavis, still at her side, bowed. "Almighty God, we believe that in your wisdom and power you are able to do all things. We ask you if it be your will, to spare the life of this young boy, Reavis Dunn. And we pray that you will grant us the strength and the wisdom we need for this moment. We place our hope in thee. In Jesus name, Amen."

Julia heard most of the voices add, "Amen".

As she opened her eyes and glanced at the children, Emmy Lou Bankston raised her hand.

Almost whispering, she said, "Miss Sutherland, if we gits bad cuts at home, Ma, she puts soot or cobwebs on the place to help stop the bleedin'."

Julia thought for a moment. Thank goodness she had not gotten the fire going yet in the stove.

"Leavis, do you think we should try it?"

"Yes'm, I guess so," he said looking as if he wanted so badly to do something, anything. "My Pa, he allus uses turkentime on a bad cut, but we ain't got none here."

"Hold his head, Leavis, and I'll get it."

The cold stove was lined with many years of accumulated soot. Julia rubbed her hand across the inside wall and then applied it gingerly to Reavis' still-bleeding head. It took several layers of this treatment before any change was noticeable.

Gradually, very gradually, the flow began to thicken and to slow. Reavis's eyes were open but he was very still. Leavis muttered unintelligibly to him.

"Leavis," Julia spoke softly, "did you say something?"

"Oh, Miss Sutherland," his words bubbled out between deep deep sobs. "Miss Sutherland, I didn't go for to do it. I know that Reavis and me, we been a-fussin' and a-scrappin' all our lifes, but I wud nefva do nothin' to hurt him, I wud nefva do..."

"It's all right, Leavis. We all know it was an accident."

At that moment Julia heard Lil' Budd's truck on the road. Bending over Reavis, she said, "Your mother is here. We are going to get you home."

For Julia and the children, concentration was difficult for the rest of the school day. She decided to let them out thirty minutes early. Some children hurried home. Others with an unusual quietness gathered outside in small groups to talk. Lou Etta and Ben Hill left school together.

Julia walked directly to see Dr. Weismann. He joined her on his front porch. "Dr. Weismann, do you know about the accident?"

"Yes, Julia, they stopped here and I took him on to Macon in my car. He's going to live. The doctor said it must have been a glancing blow, but it took a lot of stitches to close him up. He bled a lot, as head injuries do."

"What should I have done, Dr. Weismann? I have never been so frightened."

"You did just fine, Julia. And there is a plus." He smiled broadly, "Never again will there be any doubt about which twin is Reavis."

"What do you mean?"

"Well, Reavis will probably have a scar on his head for the rest of his life---perhaps a dark scar."

"Oh, how terrible. Julia felt a pang of guilt. "Perhaps I shouldn't have---"

Dr. Weismann interrupted her. "The important thing is that he will live. Mrs. Dunn is very grateful. He'll be able to come home in a few days."

Julia walked home slowly. She was extremely tired, drained. Her legs felt weak, almost numb. She decided that the events of this day had been the most challenging experience of her entire life. She wondered if Miss Potter might have handled the situation better. What would she have done? What would Rose or Mama have done? She hoped she never had to face such a trial again.

When she reached the house, Rose greeted her. "Mis' Sutherlan', Donny and Sari tol' me what happened. I'm right proud a' what you done."

"Thank you, Rose." Julia sank into a chair at the kitchen table. "Dr. Weismann said Reavis may have a dark scar. I'm sorry for that. Because of what I did, his head may look like the tail of a gray fox."

"Maybe," said Rose. "But at least he'll be a live fox."

Chapter 14--The Proposal

On Friday of that same week Bitty Budd came for a visit when he got off from the mine. As usual, he accepted Rose's invitation to stay for supper. "Rose," he said, "I heard at the mine today that Mr. Northrup's takin' sick. Real sick."

"Yes, we heard that, Bitty Budd," Rose said.

After supper Julia announced that she was going to the school to put some arithmetic problems on the blackboard for Monday morning. Bitty Budd stopped, smiled broadly and said, "I'll walk with ya Mis' Julya."

It was dusk, a warm March dusk. New green leaves were forcing the yellow tassels off the post oaks and water oaks. They lay like clumps of dusty mustard- colored worms along the edges of the road.

The two walked silently for a few minutes. Bitty Budd was turning his toothpick the long way over and over between his tongue and lips.

Julia had never seen anyone do this before. She was amused by his ability to think, walk and play with the toothpick all at the same time. Also his body often moved as though it were keeping time to music only he could hear. Occasionally he would stop, stand still and announce what he was thinking.

"Miss Julya, you see that ring around the moon up there?" Julia nodded. "It means that rain is coming; and did you know that the moon rises about fifty minutes later every night? Mos' everybody used to know that, but nowdays hardly any body remembers." He shrugged his shoulders.

"No, Bitty Budd, I did not know that. That's interesting."

"It are thet, cud'n Dick."

"Bitty Budd, tell me, who is your cousin Dick? Does he live in Chalk Creek?"

"Ma'am?"

"Your cousin, the one you refer to so often."

"I don' have no cousin, Mis' Julya. At least none 'sept'n Rose."

"Well, what do you mean when you say, 'It are that, Cud'n Dick'?"

"Do I say that?"

"Yes, you do," Julia said with a smile. "Quite often, and I wondered who he was."

Bitty Budd stopped walking, removed his toothpick and thought for several seconds. His forehead creased and he studied the ground intently. Finally, he looked up, shook his head and said, "I don't know, Mis' Julya. I reckon it jus' seems lika good thing to say. It are thet."

He nodded emphatically and replaced the toothpick. They began walking again.

A sudden, nearby owl sound startled Julia. "Was that a screech owl?"

"No'm, it's more n' likely a barn owl out huntin' rats and mice. Them screech owls make a quav-rin' moan-in' whistle like. Sometimes it's a short hoot like. But these here barn owls, they don't hoot. It's sorta a wheezy-like cry. You know, folks say owls kin turn they heads completly around. That ain't true. They cain't quite make it all the way. I figger if'n they did, well---they'd jus choke theyselves to death. But you know what?"

Julia shook her head, "What?"

"They usually stays in the same tree hole for life. An' another thang they do is they mates fa' life." At that moment Bitty Budd awkwardly encircled Julia's waist with his left arm and squeezed her to his side. His right arm fumbled to pull her closer.

Julia felt the warmth of his body, and swallowed hard. "You know a lot about owls, Bitty Budd, and animals and nature." She extracted herself from his embrace and added, "Here, let me take hold of your arm."

Turning to face her, he gripped her shoulders in his large hands. "Well, I know one thang---you're the pruttiest girl I ever seen. That's a fact. It are that Cud'n Dick."

"Thank you, Bitty Budd, you're kind." Julia tried to begin walking again, but Bitty Budd did not move.

"You're entirely welcome, Mis' Julya. I was jus' wonderin' if, if you had a sweetheart." Once it was said, encouraged by his own valor, he hurried on. "Cause if you don't, I sure would like for you n' me to be sweethearts."

At that moment Julia felt his audacity could have prompted laughter, but his sincere naiveté demanded a serious answer. She hesitated. "Bitty Budd, I truly value your friendship. You are the best checker player I've ever met, and one of the most interesting people I've ever known."

"You really think so?" he interrupted.

"Yes, I do. However, I am writing to a friend who is serving now in France with the Expeditionary Forces. We have no future plans just now, but he is a very good friend."

"You mean, you like him more 'n me." He shifted his weight and took a deep breath. "I may not have tol' you this, Mis' Julya, but las' October Pa took me to Macon to volunteer for the army. I signed all them papers an' took a lot'a tests, but they said they didn' need no more men right then. But I woulda gone."

Julia could not hurt his feelings. "Not exactly more, Bitty Budd, let's just say---in a different way. Can't you and I always be good friends?"

He didn't answer. His face was clouded. They walked in silence until they reached the school yard.

Chapter 15--Charity Afield

The next morning when Julia walked into the kitchen, she found Rose muttering to herself, as she often did. She turned and said, "Our God is 'a consumin' fire' and its been five days now since Mr. Northrup took sick. He ain't no better and some folks is sayin' it serves him right But that ain't no way to look at it, is it Mis' Sutherlan'?"

Julia shook her head.

"Like I tol' ya, Mis' Effie's never been very friendly to me, so I wuz wonderin' if yu'd mind takin' some vegetable soup an' cornbread up t' th' house if I git it ready. It looks like th' clouds is breakin' off."

"I would be glad to, Rose," Julia assured her. "Is he still paralyzed?"

"Their cook, Lottie, tol' Mis' Hawkins thet he wuz. He's always been s'sure of hisself I feel like I should git permission to do him a favor. It's a puzzlement, how some folks can make you feel they're doin' you a favor to accept a gift. I wonder if God dudn' look at us and scratch his head n' say, 'Why can't they jes' accept my Gift and say thank ya?' An' I thank you for takin' the soup."

As Julia approached the Northrup's house with Rose's offering, she noticed six or eight of Miss Effie's dresses hanging from a clothesline stretched across the upstairs porch. They had all been dyed black.

Miss Effie herself answered the door. "Oh, Miss Sutherland," she said, "I did not expect company."

"I won't come in Mrs. Northrup. Rose Wimbush sent some soup and cornbread. We were very sorry to hear about Mr. Northrup's stroke."

"Oh, yes. It is bad, but come in, he will want to see you. Ralph is upstairs now tending to him. Ralph used to tend the garden, but now he tends to Aquila." She wrung her hands and laughed nervously.

"I was planning to go in a few weeks to Hot Springs to take the waters. I had reserved a room at the Arlington Hotel and at the Fordyce Bathhouse. Now I don't suppose I can go. I am trying not to be disappointed. You know how the Good Book says, 'We must not be weary in well-doing for in due season we shall reek if we faint not'."

Reek? Julia smiled. Papa would find Miss Effie's interpretation of the Bible quite amusing.

"I will give the soup to Lottie," Mrs. Northrup said. "Go on upstairs. His room is on the front. When you come down, I want you to see some china I have been painting."

As she passed the parlor, Julia noticed that the Coca-Cola bottle was still on the mantel.

Several bedrooms opened off a wide upstairs hall. The front bedroom door was almost closed. Julia waited before knocking. She heard Mr. Northrup saying, "What's the matter, Ralph? Hurry up! I need to use the urinal."

"Jes' hol' on there Misa Northrup--hol' on--'twixt deese kivers an' yo' jamas, I's havin' troubl' findin' yo' teeter--hol' on."

"Well, Goddamn it, Ralph--you'd better find it. You were the last one who had it!"

Outside in the hallway Julia covered her mouth. She waited until it was safe to knock.

Mr. Northrup's left eye drooped and his speech was slurred, but not too hard to understand. Channels of comb marks showed where Ralph had slicked down his brown hair. Coffee and pudding were waiting on a tray nearby.

"Come in, Miss Sutherland. Nice of you to come. As you might guess, it takes a lot of patience to let them wait on me--coffee's cold, spilled in the saucer. Would you open those window shades in front?"

"Mr. Northrup, they are open."

"Well, what in God's name are those black flags flapping in the breeze? Do you see them?"

"Yes sir, I see them. I saw them as I walked up the driveway. I think they may be curtains or blankets."

She could not tell him that they are Miss Effie's dresses, already dyed black for his imminent departure.

"I don't suppose anyone has heard from Miss Potter," he said.

"No, sir, not a word. It seems very strange."

"I believe she felt that our schools down here are far inferior to what she knew. And they probably are. Perhaps that's why she left."

He rambled on for awhile about the difficulties of educating all of the children, even the poor ones with illiterate parents. His voice grew weaker and Julia felt she should leave. She said good-bye and returned to the front hall where Miss Effie was waiting for her holding a piece of china.

"This is the set of china I have been painting. That's real gold on the edges, you know."

"It's lovely, Miss Effie."

Julia thought it odd that Miss Effie's main concern over her husband's stroke seemed to be the inconvenience it had caused her. Perhaps she was someone "more to be pitied than censored."

Again Julia's gaze was caught by the dusty bottle over the fireplace, and curiosity overcame decorum. "Would you tell me about the Coca-Cola bottle on the mantel, Miss Effie?"

"Yes, dear." In a hushed tone like that of someone speaking in church, Miss Effie said, "In 1905, our little five-year-old daughter, Ione, fell ill with diphtheria. She asked for a Coca-Cola, and Aquila sent for one. She took a few sips and died with it in her hand."

Miss Effie took a lace edged handkerchief from her pocket and dabbed at the corners of her eyes. "Ione was a strong-willed child and Aquila always told her, 'I want to leave you enough money so that when I die you won't have to be nice to anybody.' But then the Lord took her home first. As the Good Book says, 'She was the apple of his eye'. Aquila's never been the same since."

Miss Effie became unusually silent and Julia thought it best to excuse herself.

As Julia left the house, she thought how sad the Northrup's lives were. She understood them better now, and why there seemed to be no happiness for either of them in that dreary, depressing place. That afternoon she wrote in her journal.

Journal Entry   March 9, 1918

Today I visited the Northrup home. No, that's wrong. Home is not the correct word. It is a house---prison, inhabited by two miserable people. Where I am living is a home.

The Northrups have let the death of their child, tragic as that is, ruin their lives.

I find myself feeling sorry for them one moment and at the same time disgusted by their small, self-centered righteousness. They could give to and be part of this community, and in so doing their own lives would be enriched.

If Aquila Northrup had memorized the words of Victor Hugo that Miss Anderson made us study in Literature class, they might have helped him. "He did not seek to drown grief in oblivion, but to exalt and dignify it by hope." Maybe nothing would have helped, maybe Mr. Northrup enjoys being miserable.

It is no wonder that Mr. Marshall was hesitant to commit himself about books or coal, or even how he wanted to help Wissie!

Chapter 16--Spring

It was a warm morning in late March. The eastern sky filled with a gentle softness of blue-gold light, like the nursery of a new day. The earth smelled mellow and full of promise as Julia and a small group walked to school. She thought of Katherine Potter and felt sorry that she left too soon to experience spring in Georgia.

Most of the boys were going barefooted now. Donny and Claud Johnson were leapfrogging ahead of the others.

Julia called to them, "Watch out boys, there is a pile of cow dung in the road."

Donny turned laughing, "That ain't no pile of cow dung, Mis' Sutherlan'. Thas' a rattlesnake. If we don' bother him, he won' bother us."

Julia and the girls stopped, looked at it for several moments, then gave the snake a wide berth as he lay defensively coiled and rattling. After they had passed, Julia turned and watched the reptile uncoil and slither into the bushes.

When they reached the school, Julia decided that she would put the fifth and sixth grade spelling words on the blackboard before she rang the school bell. As she began to write, she recognized Adam's excited, high-pitched voice even before he burst into the school room.

"Miss Julya, Miss Julya."

She turned from the board. "What is it, Adam?"

"Miss Julya, we dun found 'em---we finally found 'em!" Adam was out of breath and flushed from running.

"That's wonderful, Adam. What was it you found?"

"Oh, Miss Julya, we ben lookin' fer 'em, the whole family's ben a lookin' fer 'em ever since last summer! Ma, she's had us even clean out that ol' shed. We've looked under everything in the house at least fifty times."

The other early arrivals gathered around Julia's desk to hear more.

"Granny's jes' ben a-wastin' away," Adam went on. "Pa said last week sumpin' was gona haf to be done to hep her. And then this mawnin' he done it! He went out real early and was a-plowin' up the corn patch to git it ready for plantin'. He had made 'bout three or four rows and was jes turnin' anuthrn when he looked down and there they wuz-alayin' in the fresh dirt jes a-grinnin' up at him! He come a-runnin' to the house yellin', 'Ma, you kin eat now---I done plowed up your teeth!' Ain't that wunerful, Mis' Sutherlan'? Granny's so happy."

"Yes, Adam, it is wonderful. The thought of Granny's teeth in the fresh dirt "grinnin' up" at Ben Pendley, with his penchant for corn liquor, made it almost impossible for the young teacher to keep a straight face.

Adam paused for a short breath and continued, "Pa says they musta fallen outa her apron pocket when she wuz plantin' corn last summer and they ben a-layin' fallow all this year."

The girls giggled and the older boys laughed out loud.

Julia rapped on the desk, "We're happy, Adam, for grandmother. Now will everyone please take your seats?"

As the children settled down and began to work, Julia was thinking of what a cheerful, happy young boy Adam was. He had not missed a day of school since she came to Chalk Creek. He seemed especially interested in learning and wanted to do even more than was required of him.

In fact, Julia thought, all her students, with the proper encouragement and consistent teaching, could make valuable contributions to society in spite of their hardships. She felt there was great potential in these children, and she realized she was enjoying her job as teacher.

The excitement that Adam's announcement had brought to the classroom was heightened all week by the news that a traveling medicine show was due to arrive in Chalk Creek on Saturday night. Large signs had been posted on the screen door of Hawkins store and on the side of the barber shop and on several trees around town announcing the performance.

MEDICINE SHOW
The One and Only
Dr. Malcolm Freemont, Esq.
Featuring his niece the Beautiful and Talented
Miss Teressa Tidwell
ADMISSION: Adults 10 cents   children free
Dr. Freemont's Amazing Elixir of Life
will be available for a special price
of only $1.00
Don't   Miss   It

At supper Rose asked, "Clarence, kin we go?"

"I suppose so, Rose," Clarence said. "The childrun might l-l-like it. Don't 'member one comin' to Ch-C-Chalk Creek before."

"Mis' Sutherlan', you wanna go with us?" Rose asked.

"Yes. I think I'd like that, Rose. I've never been to a medicine show."

Saturday night was comfortably warm and at seven o'clock it was still light enough to see Dr. Freemont's gypsy-like wagon situated in the wide dirt area in front of the barber shop. Bales of hay had been arranged in rows for seating. A platform extended from the back of the wagon and from this Dr. Freemont welcomed the crowd, told several jokes and for what seemed to be an interminable time extolled the value of the **Elixir of Life**. He sold six bottles before he introduced the beautiful Teressa. A green shiny curtain parted enough for Teressa to step onto the platform.

Julia estimated that this pretty child, with heavy rouge, lip paint and eye make-up, her blond hair curled and be-ribboned, could not be more than fourteen. She was wearing a low cut, rather short red dress, red stockings, red shoes and an imitation diamond choker.

She began her entertaining by singing The Mademoiselle from Armentieres. When she reached the "Par-le-voo" part she had one hand on her swaying hips and gestured with the other for the audience to join with her. She concluded by kicking her leg rather high. The men clapped, loving it. Obviously offended, Sarah Hawkins got up and stalked off. A few minutes later Jimmy Hawkins reluctantly followed her.

Teressa then gave a not-too-bad rendition of the Habanera aria from Carmen, did a little tap dance using a tambourine, and ended her program with patriotic fervor by singing My Buddy, Pack Up Your Troubles and Over There. On the last strains of "and we won't be back til it's over, over there" she dramatically unrolled an American flag she had extracted from between her breasts. With one accord the audience was hers, and Dr. Freemont sold five more bottles of his Elixir.

Mr. and Mrs. Mobley sat next to Julia. Mrs. Mobley whispered to Mr. Mobley, who got up, went to the front and bought a bottle of Dr. Freemont's cure-all.

Mrs. Mobley explained to Julia, "Lou Etta's not been feeling "up to par" lately. She's right pale and don't eat right."

Before Dr. Freemont began telling jokes again, Julia asked Mr. Mobley about the fire tower and his job.

"Would you like to climb it sometime?" he asked. "Children are not allowed, and most folks aren't inter-rested, but if you'd like to see what it's like, I'll take you."

"I would love to! Perhaps from up there I could get a better idea of what the mine looks like."

"Yes, you could. What about tomorrow after dinner?"

"I'll be there."

Mrs. Mobley invited Julia to come and have dinner before climbing the tower. This was her first invitation other than the Northrups. Because no one else had the room or wanted to board the teacher, moving to other homes in the community had never materialized and Julia was glad.

As the crowd was leaving the medicine show, a family Julia had met at church, Mr. and Mrs. Dewey Blane and their ten children from over in Centerville, filed out in front of her. Mr. Blane turned and said quietly but boastfully to his wife, "Come on Lois, look at that full moon, let's get on home, tonight's the night---I can feel it."

Julia heard Mrs. Blane plead under her breath, "Oh, Lord, no! Not again."

She laughed silently at Mrs. Blane's petition and made her way through the thinning crowd to join Rose and Clarence.

As they went up the steps at home Sari said, "Ma, I wanta be jes' like that Teressa when I grow up. Wad'n she beau-ti-ful!"

Clarence shook his head and mumbled, "We shouldna' gone. It's a g-g-good thing revival's starting next week."

Before she got in bed, Julia drew aside her window curtain and looked at the clean swept yard bathed in moonlight. It was a beautiful night. How far away Conway seemed, much more than 150 miles, and farther still the barren fields of France. In the distance she heard coon hounds howling, baying, yapping and coming closer. Now she heard men calling to one another and running very close behind the dogs. As they came nearer, the Wimbush hounds growled and bayed but did not leave the yard. Gradually the sounds faded and the night was still.

On Sunday morning Rose served everyone a cup of her "spring tonic". She said it was made by boiling the bark and roots of the sassafras tree and would work as well as that one-dollar elixir.

Although Pearl Mobley had fixed a dinner of fried chicken, stewed corn, rice, beans, ham and biscuits for Julia, she noticed that Lou Etta merely picked at her food. As Mama would say, "her eyes looked weak" and Julia hoped that the young girl was not coming down with influenza or some other illness.

That afternoon when they began to climb the tower, Benton Mobley cautioned, "Don't look down, Mis' Sutherlan' and you won't have no trouble. This is not a real high tower."

It seemed high enough to Julia, but the view from the little platform at the top was worth the climb.

"Oh, Mr. Mobley, tell me what I am seeing!"

Julia could identify the ribbon of road she had traveled with the Budds from the train track to the Wimbush place. She could spot the roofs of the Hawkins' store, the Northrup house and several others, but turning in the other direction produced a sight like nothing she had ever seen before. A flat area of pines and hardwoods in poor-looking soil would suddenly open with a sheer drop of perhaps forty to sixty feet. The walls of these cliffs, which formed an irregular circle, were white as chalk, as was the floor, extending in some places as much as a half mile.

Pointing to the nearest one, Mr. Mobley said, "That's Mine Number Four. You can see part of the narrow gauge track running along the bottom. 'Bout thirty feet, or half way up, you can see that shelf of clay that's bein' mined. Way down there on the bottom you can spot some wheelbarrows the men left out   yesterday."

"Now what is that one I can see in the distance?"

"That's an old abandoned mine. It was used back in the late 1800's, but not any more. That area to the left of it, that flat clearing, that's where the overburden was removed and it ain't grown back much, just around the edges."

Julia looked at it very hard. Why did she feel that she had seen it before? "Does anyone ever go there, Mr. Mobley? Is it used for anything?"

"No'm. There's an ol' loggin' road runnin' almost up to it-- lots of big rocks in that area, but it's pretty isolated now. Before the clay ran out, it was one of the deepest ones around. You see that pit off to the right over there? That's the one Big Budd slid into and messed up his hip. He's tough as whitleather,--it woulda' kilt any body else."

Julia's eyes lingered on the abandoned mine until they began their descent.

As she reached the bottom of the ladder, suddenly she remembered. It was Wissie's drawing. That's where she had seen that place! But why would Wissie know about it? Why would she have gone there? And how? Wissie's drawing showed two stick people. Did Miss Potter ever go there? Did she take Wissie? There were so many unanswered questions.

Late that afternoon Julia wrote letters to Mama and Papa, and to Stephen Whitfield. She also wrote to Amelia Sanders, a former student from college, who was teaching now in Macon. She asked Amelia about the possibility of getting information from the Institute of Mental Retardation. Mr. Marshall had not given her a report on Wissie's testing.

Chapter 17--Hinged Ladders

In the late afternoon of an early spring day, Julia sat at the kitchen table with Rose who was cleaning and filling the kerosene lamps and trimming the wicks. Donny was milking and Sari was on the back porch reading. They had talked of various things and then Rose said, "Mis' Sutherlan', may I ast you sumpin?"

"Certainly, Rose, what is it?"

"Well---I've heer'd you speak about yo' Mama's help---Herbert, n'Eva, n'Sallie Fannie, and what I wuz wonderin' wuz", she seemed hesitant to continue, "are you ever sceer'd of 'em? There never has been any of 'em in Chalk Creek, as I know of. I never have known any of 'em. Clarence said there are several that comes an works at the mine, but they don' live near here. Are you ever sceer'd?"

"No, Rose. Never once. Let me tell you how it is. I love them and I hope they love me. Eva and Sallie Fannie are like benevolent aunts to me. They have corrected me when I was a child and many times tolerated my rebellious behavior. Herbert has on more than one occasion, rescued me from trees that were easy to climb but too scary for me to descend.

When I was a little girl I loved to follow him to the barns and watch him do the milking or gather the eggs in the chicken house. I remember one of my proudest days was when he gave me a brush and let me 'help him' paint the picket fence around Mama's flower garden.

"I can think of two occasions that might explain to you how things are between us.

"One night word reached Papa that Sheriff Roberts was holding Earl Neal's boy in the county jail for being drunk and disorderly. Papa dressed and drove the twelve miles over to the county seat. He walked into the jail and asked to take the Neal boy home. The Sheriff said he thought it would teach the boy a lesson to spend the night in jail. I don't know how he knew it but Herbert told me later that this is what happened.

"Papa said, 'Well, Sheriff, if you'll just tell me what the fine is, I'll settle up with you, take him home and let him sleep it off there.'

"One of the deputies looked at Papa and said, 'Nigga lover---are you a nigga lover?'

"Herbert said, Papa calmly paid the fine, waited until they brought Sedrick to him, then turned to the deputy and said, 'Yes, for your information, I love this boy. I've known him since he was a baby, and he's no worse and no better than one of my own boys.' Then he drove him home.

"Another incident, that completes the picture, happened several years ago. I was away at school but Mama told me about it. It seems that Papa had a distant relative, a third cousin everyone called Shug. She was not a very pretty girl and the family was relieved when an older widower from Alabama married her and they went to Alabama to live. Two sons and a daughter were born, then several years later the man died. Word came to Papa that the man had left her destitute. She had nothing. Feeling that family ought to help family, he offered Shug a house, some acreage and a mule if she and her boys wanted to try to farm. They moved in and things went along well for a few years. Then one morning in spring, the boys were about sixteen and seventeen years old, Papa was making his rounds of the farms. As he approached Shug's place he saw her in the field behind the mule plowing, the daughter walking behind her was dropping seeds into the furrows. He stopped and asked Shug where the boys were. They had gone off, she did not know where. Papa drove into town and in front of the blacksmith shop he saw them. As he described the scene, 'two tall strapping young white bucks in a huddle with three smaller Negroes passing a pint bottle and shooting dice.' He stopped the car, approached them, and in no uncertain terms explained to them that if they did not get home, help their mother make something of that place he would put them out. As he returned to his car, the boys yelled at Papa, 'We'll git you ol'man. We'll git you! You'll see.' "

Rose had finished her job with the lamps and sat down by Julia to hear the rest of the story.

"Are you sorry you asked, Rose?"

"Oh no'm, go on with the story."

"Well Mama said that several weeks had gone by. They had forgotten the incident. Then late one Saturday afternoon she and Papa heard in the driveway loud cracking noises, drunken yelling, laughing and name calling. 'Oh Billy--Yeh, Billy, com'on out'cher you ol'fool--come on out'cher. I'm gonna flick yo' thing off and take yo' manhood away.' The boys each had a long black leather bull-whip which they flipped and snapped as they staggered up the driveway breaking off small limbs and branches of the nandinas and the camellias. Mama said she was terrified. She begged Papa not to go out. He said he would go for the Sheriff. He was afraid they would set fire to the house or one of the barns. Before Papa could get to the car they cornered him, one whip completely encircled him and he was thrown to the ground. Just at that moment Herbert and Trummie Neal came into the drive from the Gypsy Woods. Herbert was able to grab the end of the other whip as it was aimed at him and he knew exactly how to use it. They drove the boys out of the yard and all the way back to the road. The Sheriff did send them off---this time to jail.

"Papa has always said that goodness comes wrapped in every color skin and laziness and meanness come wrapped the same way.

"To answer your question, Rose, no I've never been afraid of any of Papa's hands. Mama has very little patience with some of them whom she feels are lazy, but we depend on each other. Like a hinged ladder, one side can't stand very well without the other."

Donny came in with the pail of milk and Sari followed him. It was beginning to get dark. "I'll put the grits on now", said Rose.

Chapter 18--
Visit with Dr. Weismann

After school on Monday, Julia walked to Hawkins store to mail her letters. A brief one from Papa was waiting for her. Standing near the store she read:

Dear Julia,

There is not much to report from Conway this week. We have had no recent letters from George. Your mother is worried that William will enlist after his 18th birthday in June.

Julia, I sense from your letters that you are concerned about Mama's feelings for you. Remember this: clouds may veil the sun, even darken it, but the light is unchangeable. Our love for you is like that.

Your loving father,
W.A.Sutherland

Julia remembered Mama's curt goodbye and said to herself, "No. No, Mama doesn't feel that kind of love for me."

"Miss Sutherland, hello." Startled from her thoughts, Julia quickly turned and saw Dr. Weismann sitting in a rocker on his front porch.

"Do you have time for a visit? My wife is resting."

Julia accepted the other chair and commented on a stack of books at his feet. In the pile was Merivale's <u>General History of Rome</u>, <u>From Chaucer to Tennyson</u> and <u>Walks and Talks in the Geological Field</u>.

"These look like interesting titles, Dr. Weismann. You obviously like to read."

"Yes," he said, "I enjoy reading. I have a lot of time now. These are sent to me from Chautauqua, N. Y.. I have been a member of the Literary and Scientific Circle for almost four years now. The books are exchanged periodically."

"It sounds like a very good program."

"It is. I have enjoyed it. But I suppose there is a possible danger in all this reading."

"What do you mean, Dr. Weismann? What danger could there be in reading?"

"Well," he said thoughtfully, "perhaps, especially in a town like Chalk Creek, we begin to see ourselves as the cultured elite, a sort of ruling class---a feeling of educational piety if you will. I don't know, but it's hard not to feel a certain superiority."

"But," Julia said, "as a professional man, you already are superior. Is that wrong?"

"Maybe," he smiled as he knocked his pipe on the porch railing to empty it. "Perhaps I should not say this to you, a teacher, but I am not sure that the means to this community's salvation is knowledge."

"Oh, what then?"

"I expect you'll come to find, in most of them, a great lack of motivation, almost a depression---as though they moved about slowly, back and forth, in separate cages."

"Is the lack of motivation due to a lack of expectation?" Julia asked, "Do they fail to hope for something better? Is there not energy in hope? If not knowledge, then what do you think it would take to create changes?"

"I don't know." He gazed into the distance, an aura of sweet sadness about him. "I believe it was A. A. Proctor who wrote:

'The hopes that lost in some far distance seen,
May be the truer life, and this the dream'."

"That's beautiful, Dr. Weismann." Julia was thinking that those lines would fit the Northrups well.

"I can tell that you are not from the South," Julia said. "How long have you lived in Chalk Creek?"

"We moved here in 1914 after the passage of the Harrison Narcotics Act. You see, for the first time then, morphine and its opiate cousins were illegal."

He shifted in his chair and continued, "I trained in Boston and was offered an associate professorship at Harvard Medical

School, but my wife, who was very proud of the fact that she was from Virginia, was miserably unhappy. So, we moved to Richmond but she was not happy there. So we tried Atlanta, then Macon."

Julia said, "That was a lot of moving."

Dr. Weismann nodded and said, "As you probably have guessed, I am Jewish, and although my wife is not, we were not as accepted in any of these places as she felt we should have been. By then our son had been born and she was having a lot of pain, first her back, then her jaw, head and neck. I could not stand to see her suffer. I prescribed medication for pain."

Julia nodded and said, "I can understand that."

"After morphine and opiates were made illegal," Dr. Weismann said, "I gave up my practice, and we moved here. I have a pharmacist friend in Macon who helps me get the medicines. My recurring nightmare is that I may die before she does."

He took a leather pouch from his coat pocket and refilled his pipe. His dark brown eyes looked sadly at something a long way off.

"I had always wanted to feel that I was in control, in charge of my life. I decided when I was young that I wanted to be a doctor--not so much because I wanted to help people, but because I could tell them what was best for them and perhaps see that they did it. I went to school where I wanted to go. I got all the degrees I wanted. I pretty well mapped out where I wanted to live and how. Then....."

His words stopped. His gaze shifted a bit and he took a long draw on his pipe.

"Then, one day life grabs you by the nape of the neck and shakes you, like a dog shaking a rag, and you realize you are no longer in control and probably never were, no more than a fly inside a train car controls where he is going. There were a lot of things I wanted to accomplish with my time on this earth. I wanted to be the engineer of that train. Somehow, somewhere---I lost control. The choices we make in life seem to make us."

Julia waited a moment to see if she should speak. "On our place back home, one of the tenant families had their eleventh baby last fall. The mother named this child Des-tinee. One day I asked Maude why she chose this name for her baby. 'Oh,' she told me, d'preacher, he say, *dey's a des-tinee what shapes our ends*, and dis'here baby sho' dun shaped mine!'"

The doctor laughed out loud, then asked, "Are you suggesting, Miss Julia, that you believe in fate, predestination?"

"Well, I don't know what label I would put on it, but I do believe that God has a best plan for our lives. But I suppose that by our choices we can mess up that grand plan. Wasn't it Thomas Carlyle who wrote, 'the Ideal is in thyself, the impediment, too, is in thyself,'?"

Smoke curled from his pipe. "Perhaps," he said quietly.

Julia continued, "My father has always said that of all men, a farmer learns very quickly that he is at the mercy of forces beyond his control."

"Yes, I suppose so," the doctor mused, "I think I would not have made a good farmer."

Julia laughed as she rose to leave. "You were just too smart to be a farmer, Dr. Weismann."

"Please come again."

"I will."

Walking up the hill toward home, Julia's thoughts would not leave Dr. Weismann. Here was a brilliant, kind, capable man, bound like a prisoner to a situation that he himself, out of compassion, had created.

Julia decided that he and Tabatha Ruth Welborn, the Gazelle, were both prisoners here in Chalk Creek. Earlier today she had spoken with Tabatha about the up-coming school picnic.

Tabitha had a pretty face, a sweet and pleasant disposition and was considerate of others. Her weight contributed to her problems. She moved slowly and with difficulty.

Julia remembered their conversation. She had said to her, "Tabitha Ruth, I hope you are planning to go to the picnic this Friday. School will be out early and children from Gatesville and Cadenton will be there. You might meet some nice young people your age." Because her schooling had been interrupted so often by illness in the family or lack of a teacher, Julia estimated that Tabatha Ruth at seventeen was only on a fourth to sixth grade level. She seemed to have no friends and her mother usually walked with her to school.

"No'm. Mama says she don' feel like goin' and she don' want me to go nowhere by myself. She says sumpin' might happen to me."

Julia had thought a moment and then asked, "Tabitha Ruth, have you ever wondered what will happen to you if you don't get out and meet some people outside of Chalk Creek?"

"Well, I never thought much about it. I reckon I'll jes' stay here and take care of Mama and Pa. I'm all they got. My sister, she married a man over in Union when his wife died, and she's heppin' him raise his five younguns."

"Tabitha Ruth, you can go with me. I'll walk you home. You would enjoy meeting some other young people."

"No'm--thank you Mis' Sutherlan', Mama, she don' want me to go."

By the time Julia reached the yard she had decided that she would not allow herself to live her life like Dr. Weismann or Tabatha Ruth.

There are many kinds of prisons. Some that circumstances make for us, like Wissie. But some we make for ourselves, and some that we let other people make for us. Had Miss Potter felt that Chalk Creek was a prison she must escape?

Chapter 19--Eppen's Loss

Apri Fool's Day was on Monday of the next week. When Julia came home that afternoon Rose was not in the kitchen and there were no signs of supper being prepared. The children had not waited for her to leave school and they were not in the yard or house. Clarence had told her that "when the new leaves on the oak trees are as big as squirrel's ears, it's time to plant corn," but he was not out checking on his newly planted rows. It was all very unusual. Julia wondered if it could be a joke. After about an hour she heard their voices outside. Rose was saying, "I jes' cain't understan' anybody bein' that mean and low down."

Clarence said, "It's h-h-h-hard to believe anybody livin' in Chalk Creek woulda' done it."

Julia met them in the kitchen. Donny was dripping wet. "What's happened, Clarence?"

Rose said, "Donny, go put on some dry clothes and hang them wet ones on the porch railin'. I'll wash 'em later."

Clarence said, "Mis' Sutherlan' you gotta let R-R-Rose tell ya." He left the kitchen and walked toward the privy, shaking his head.

Whatever it was that had happened had saddened and affected each of them.

Rose crumpled paper into the stove, added wood, and began supper preparations as she talked.

"Mis' Sutherlan', when Clarence went to Hawkins store to git me some thread and some coffee, Jimmy Hawkins tol' him that Eppen hadn' been to town all mornin'. He walks them geese you know ever mornin' and they grazes along the road side. Well Clarence thought maybe he better check on 'im and went to his place. He said what he seen nearly broke his heart."

Julia sat down at the table to hear more.

"Eppen was a-settin' on his back steps slowly rockin' and rockin'---back and forth---softly moanin' over and over and over, 'Shirley---oh Shirley, my Shirley'. He was holdin' Shirley's bloody head and neck in his hand, rubbin' and strokin' the feathers, first one way, then the other way. Blood was dried all over Eppen's hands."

"Oh no." Julia said. "What happened?"

Rose rushed on, almost crying as she spoke. "Mis' Sutherlan', somebody during the night had wrung that goose's neck. Clarence said that Goodness and Mercy were settin' at his feet, but Shirley's body wadn' no where to be seen. He looked all around and at first he figgered a fox don got 'er. But if it'd been a fox, it'd drug all of 'er into the woods. Then he said he figgered somebody wuz powerful hongry and wanted a good dinner, some tramp more n' likely maybe passin' by, but then he seen drops of blood leadin' from the side of the house goin' all the way to the well. You see, them geese, they usually roosts under his house, sometimes in a tree, but usually under the house."

Julia nodded.

By now the fire was doing well and Rose was patting and shaping biscuits. "Eppen's well is the best 'un in the whole county. I 'member when his Pa dug it. I wuz jus' a young girl an' a dowser come through Chalk Creek. He carried a sign thet said, 'No water, no pay'. Instead of a forked stick he used two L-shaped rods. I 'member he held 'm out chest high, like he wuz gonna' shoot somebody, an' he walked all over thet yard---up one side, down the other. All of a sudden, them rods they begun to swing inward. When they crossed, he hollar'd out, 'Dig here!' and sure 'nuff, Eppen's all'us had plenty of water."

Julia smiled at the image of the dowser.

"Clarence said he thought one person might be mean enough to wring a goose's neck, but it probably would take two or more to think up ruinin' a man's well water. Mis' Sutherlan', they wuz jes' like his cheerun." Rose put ham in the skillet to fry, stirred the grits and slid the pan of biscuits in the oven.

"Clarence come on home and tol' me what had happened. I fixed Eppen some dinner and as soon as Donny and Sari come in we we took it to him. We let Donny down the well in the bucket and sure 'nuff, he fished out Shirley. I don' know how long it'll take fa' that water to be fittin' to drink. We buried Shirley near the back steps."

"I feel so sorry for poor Eppen," Julia said.

"Eppen loaded his shot gun and said he's gon' set up all night---that he'd kill anybody thet come on his place. Bitty Budd said he'd take Eppen some water and stay with 'im tonight. Bitty Budd's slow to anger, Mis' Sutherlan', and he won't let Eppen kill nobody, but they sho could scare the fire out of 'em."

"I thought geese were usually aggressive and noisy," Julia said. "I'm surprised anyone could slip up on them without Eppen hearing something."

"Yes'm. We wuz, too."

"Is there some sheriff or law enforcement officer that would look into this?"

"No'm. The nearest law is over at Union, and he'd jes' say it was probably a boyhood prank. But them geese is Eppen's life. He loves 'em. Clarence said he wouldn't put it pass them ol' Cochrane boys to pull such a stunt. If Durrell had been a beatin' on 'em and they wuz drinkin', they jes might come through those woods a-lookin' fa' fun. We'll never know fa' sure, but that's more n' likely whut happened."

"Having met Durrell Cochrane," Julia said, "I agree that his sons might be mean enough to do such a terrible thing."

"But, Rose," Julia continued, "I can see one bright spot. Goodness and Mercy were not only sitting at Eppen's feet, but also, because of friends like you and Clarence and Bitty Budd, they will be with him all the days of his life."

"Well, I hope so, Mis' Sutherlan'."

Julia did not say it aloud to Rose, but she wondered if Durrell Cochrane had threatened Miss Potter with his ax. Had he frightened her badly enough that she just suddenly left town?

Chapter 20--Caged, but Free

Julia found another bright spot in Chalk Creek. Mrs. Carrie Alston lived next door to Dr. Weismann, in the third house from Hawkins General Store. Hers was one of the few homes in Chalk Creek where Julia had not visited. Mrs. Alston had no children, but Rose had said that she 'knew everything about everybody' and Julia felt she might learn some things from her about Wissie's background.

As yet Mr. Marshall had not brought Julia a report on Wissie's testing and she had heard nothing from Amelia Sanders about the Institute in Macon. She was beginning to wonder if perhaps Wissie was more emotionally stunted from her father's meanness than she was retarded.

Rose sent a pan of warm biscuits to Miss Carrie and Julia thought as she walked along that Mama would have done this, too. She realized she was beginning to see qualities in Rose that reminded her of Mama---qualities that in Mama had seemed like foibles, but in Rose were like strengths.

Two large fig bushes flanked either side of Mrs. Alston's front steps. They were loaded with tiny, immature fruit. "Ripe by June," Julia thought.

In answer to Julia's knock, a sweet voice called, "Come in, come in."

The door was unlocked. In the center of a small room, a radiant smile encased in a frail, bent body sat in a wheelchair. "Oh, I am so glad you came to see me," Mrs. Alston said. "Dr. Weismann has told me about you, Miss Sutherland, and I have been hoping you would come. Do sit down. Oh, biscuits, how nice, would you put them on the kitchen table?"

When Julia returned she noticed Mrs. Alston was crocheting what appeared to be adult-sized bootees. The last two fingers on both her hands were bent into her palms and the other fingers were swollen at the joints and crooked.

"I call these foot warmers. Lots of folks like to sleep in them." She held up a pink pair and said, "I made these for you."

"Oh, thank you," Julia said.

"I knew you would come. I also like to make quilts when I can get enough scraps and backing. The one over there on the sofa I'm trying to finish for a wedding present."

She smiled and added, "I don't know who for yet, but the Lord will send someone by the time I get the fabric. I like to use Ballard Obelisk flour sacking for the backs. It doesn't shrink."

Pointing to a chair, she said, "Sit here by me and tell me about yourself, Miss Sutherland. You are already beloved by people in Chalk Creek. I'm so glad you are here."

"I'm glad to be here, Mrs. Alston," Julia said.

"Do call me Carrie."

"All right, Miss Carrie. My home is in Conway, a farming community, where cotton and peaches are the major crops. I have an older brother who is serving in France, a brother at the University of Georgia and a very young brother at home. I am the oldest of three girls."

"You are so fortunate, dear, to have a large family. My precious husband, the love of my life, worked for the railroad and was killed in a train accident two years after we married. We had no children, but as the Psalmist says 'God setteth the solitary in families', and the good people of Chalk Creek have become my family. They're always doing something for me, like Rose sending me biscuits."

Julia smiled and nodded.

"After Gerald's death, I stayed on here with my parents and took care of them. I never really thought about being crippled myself. Others I watched get older and fail, but I thought it would not happen to me."

She gave a soft contented laugh. "Now I can't use my hands much, my knees and hips have given out and the worst thing, my eyes are beginning to fail."

"I'm sorry to hear that, Miss Carrie."

"But I have been so blessed. I have quiet time to read my Bible and my favorite poet, Whittier. Every day is different. Someone comes to see me and I know, if for nothing else, God can use me to listen to people."

"And that," said Julia, "can be very helpful."

Julia had planned to ask her about Wissie, but at this point she wanted to hear more about Carrie Alston. "Miss Carrie, were you from Chalk Creek originally?"

"Oh no, dear, I was sixteen when Sherman marched through Georgia. My parents lost everything---our home, my father's business, everything. Our money was worth-less. My father moved us here when the Clay Company started mining. The company has been a godsend for all of these people. Those were desperate times. I met my husband after we moved here. How do you like Chalk Creek?"

"It's fine Miss Carrie, but I wish there were more interest from the people in the school and in other community improvements."

"I know dear, but you see, most of these people were born into the terrible, grinding poverty of those years after the war between the states. They had nothing. First you must think of your own survival and that of your family. Only then are you free to think of the community."

"I can understand that, Miss Carrie, and I realize how fortunate my family has been but---"

"Our past is always with us," Miss Carrie said. Even generations later, its still with us. It's who we are, a part of us, and so much a part of our present it's like an egg stirred into cornmeal. We cannot separate the two. It colors our thinking and our decision making."

She stopped crocheting and looked at Julia. "The future is like a dark velvet curtain that shuts off our view beyond this very moment. It's up to your generation now to make those improvements happen. You know those lines from Whittier that say,

> *'Who may not strive, may yet fulfill*
> *The harder task of standing still,*
> *And good but wished with God is done.'*

I do a lot of wishing and praying."

Julia smiled. "If you could have one wish---other than being made well again--- what would it be, Miss Carrie?"

"Well, let's see. I wouldn't waste a wish on being made well again. Someday I shall be free of this imprisoning body. I have thought about how much I would like to see those cherry trees in bloom, the ones in Washington that Mrs. Taft asked the Japanese to send us. They must be beautiful this time of the year. And I think it would be exciting to see one of those moving picture shows, like The Birth of a Nation.

"But I think what I would most like, would be to hear Rev. Billy Sunday preach. He seems to be not only devout, but also practical and funny. You know he used to be a major league baseball player. He was the one who said, 'Going to church doesn't make you a Christian any more than going to a garage makes you an automobile'."

She laughed. "So often he hits the nail squarely on the head, and since I can't go to church I like that thought."

"My wish right now, Miss Carrie, is that I could help one of my students, Wissie Cochrane."

"Oh Wissie!" Miss Carrie shook her head, "Poor child."

"Do you know anything about her, or her family? Her skin is very fair and I have noticed bruises on her wrists and arms. Her father talks so mean to her and I am concerned that he may be mistreating her. I don't know what to think, or what I can do."

"I'm afraid I don't know much about the Cochranes," Miss Carrie said. "They stay to themselves. He has a reputation for drinking and probably making whiskey. He's never been able to keep a steady job. His first wife died quite suddenly and I feel very sorry for the present Mrs. Cochrane.

"Died suddenly?" Julia asked. "Was she ill?"

"Well, no one knew it, if she was. He came into town one day and told Jimmy Hawkins she died the week before. Apparently, she's buried somewhere on his place."

"Can that be done, legally, Miss Carrie?"

"I really don't know, but it was done, and no one seems to know anything about it."

"My Goodness!"

"Then the next thing we knew, he'd gone off and brought back from Jenkins County this present wife, Wissie's mother. As I said, they stay pretty much to themselves."

"Well, he's a strange one, strange and scary, and I don't like the bruises on Wissie."

"Perhaps you could talk to Mr. Marshall about it."

"Yes, I think I shall." Julia nodded

"You be careful. When I think of the Cochranes I think of what my husband used to say. He hoped all of our children would be boys."

Julia looked puzzled. "Boys? Why, Miss Carrie?"

"Because, he said, a girl's life is so limited, so defined by whatever her husband is, and provides. Mrs. Cochrane is a prime example."

"I had never thought of it that way, Miss Carrie, but if that is true, I'm not sure I want to marry."

"Oh, yes you do, dear. Just select carefully."

"Miss Carrie, I have another question. I am curious about Miss Potter. Did you get to know her?"

"No, dear, she never came to see me. I gathered that she was unhappy here in Chalk Creek, but I do not understand her sudden disappearance. I think it was a very unseemly way to behave."

"Yes, I suppose." Unseemly Julia thought, but more important perhaps, unexplained. She stood and said, "I must go, but I hope I may come again. Thank you for the pretty foot warmers."

"You are more than welcome, my dear."

"Miss Carrie, I do wish that all good, virtuous people could be as merry as you are. Pious people who act sad all the time and look as though they just swallowed a sour pickle, make being bad seem like much more fun than being good."

Miss Carrie laughed, "You know when we are young we don't realize how important it is to live each day joyfully, because today may be all we have of tomorrow. Psalm 130 says 'I wait for the Lord, my soul doth wait, and in his word do I hope'. That's my watchword."

"You are wise and merry, Miss Carrie. I have enjoyed my visit."

As she left the house Julia thought that Carrie Alston was as physically caged as a canary, but spiritually and emotionally she was free, alive---soaring. Julia hoped that if she lived that long, she could be like Miss Carrie.

Jimmy Hawkins spotted Julia passing the store. He ran out waving a letter. It was from Papa, enclosing another from Stephen Whitfield.

Julia fought down a feeling of excitement. She tried to remember what Rose had said during one of their talks. "Women will never get rid of waiting for the right man." She did not want to let herself fall into that trap. Carrie Alston was right---she did not want her life circumscribed, defined by a man. She forced herself to read Papa's letter first.

He wrote that things were generally going well in Conway. They missed her.

The new occurrence was Ruth's being sent home from boarding school with a bad ear infection that turned out to be mastoiditis. Dr. Walter Byrd came down from Atlanta on the train. He decided an operation was necessary. With your Mother assisting him, he used the breakfast room table as an operating table and things went well. Julia, your Mother was a real trouper. Dr. Byrd spent the night and we got him on the morning train back to Atlanta. Ruth is doing quite well, but I thought you should know.

We love you,
W. A. Sutherland

Stephen's letter touched her heart in ways she had never felt before. He wrote,

I have seen men asleep marching and awake marching. We wear our boots day and night. Many of the men have Trench Fever caused by lice. The shelling of the trenches is at times incessant, as often as three blasts a minute all day. Two nights ago I was sitting on a log after fierce shelling had ended, sitting in the dark talking with my Captain. We spoke of the difficulty some of the southern soldiers, soldiers with names like "Pea-eye Smoot" and "Shoot Higgins", are having saluting the Negro officers we sometimes pass in the villages and

183

when our companies meet on the road. We also talked of the men who had been wounded, of home, of our plans and hopes for the future as we shared a tin of potted meat. After we finished, he took out a cigarette, lit a match and a sniper's bullet hit him between the eyes. He fell backwards, the only sound was the crack of the rifle. Had he lived, I think we might have become very good friends. Now I have been given a field promotion to Captain and will try to take his place. This whole interminable hell reminds me of Dante's virtuous Pagans who live "in desire without hope". My hope, my constant prayer is that God will let me live to get home to you. Rumor has it that General Ludendorff will mount a huge offensive in the spring. If so, there would undoubtedly be an Allied counterattack, probably near St. Mehiel or the [CENSORED] Forest. I hope you are well.

I think of you often.

Most sincerely,
Stephen M. Whitfield

Tears welled in her eyes and ran down her cheeks. She was surprised by her concern for his safety. She bit her lip and angrily prayed, "Oh, God, when will this hideous war be over?"

Chapter 21--A Long Week

As any teacher will attest, there are some weeks of teaching that never seem to end. For Julia Sutherland, the second week of April was just such a time.

The weather was very nice, sunny, and not too warm. The children were attending regularly, and she was enjoying them. Because very little farming was done in this area they were not having to stop school and help with the spring planting. She hoped to accomplish a great deal between now and June. She understood now the words she had often heard Mama say, "Time is the teacher's currency".

Each school morning always began with Bible story and the Lord's prayer. Even the youngest ones were able now to repeat most of the phrases. On Monday of this particular week during a geography and history assignment for the older students and a reading session with the younger ones, Adam Pendley raised his hand and asked to be excused.

"Yes, Adam. Hurry back."

Hallie Maude Hardy was reading <u>The Three Billy Goats Gruff</u> from the Elson Reader, Book One.

"Once there were three Billy goats. They were all named Gruff."

Julia whispered, "Pay attention, Melvin. I may call on you next."

"Every day they went up a hill to eat tha grass and grow fat. They had to go over a little brook-----"

At that point the door flew open, Adam rushed in and between sobs, Julia deciphered his words, "Oh, Mis' Sutherlan', Mis' Sutherlan', what am I gonna do? My Pa'll kill me---oh, oh---Mis' Sutherlan', what kin I do?"

"Calm down, Adam, and tell me what has happened." He was wild-eyed and trembling and Julia realized immediately his glasses were not on his round face. Twelve children sat perfectly still, listening.

"Mis' Sutherlan'," Adam sobbed. "I leant over to look, and my glasses fell in. Pa'll kill me!"

"Now, Adam, that's not going to happen. We'll just get your glasses out." Immediately the sobbing stopped. His eyes widened.

"No!" Adam shook his head. "Oh no, Mis' Suth- erlan', we can't do that!" He paused, then said emphatically, "There's Be-excused in there!"

Julia tried to keep a straight face. She did not want to embarrass Adam. When the door opened a second time and Gilbert Dudley Marshall, dressed in his dark suit and tie, stepped into the room he found twelve children and their teacher loudly laughing, some stomping their feet and the teacher hugging Adam.

Silence moved through the room from the back to the front and Mr. Marshall asked, "What's going on here, Miss Sutherland?"

Julia rose. "I'm glad you have come, Mr. Marshall. We have somewhat of an emergency. Adam Pendley's expensive glasses fell in the privy and we do need to retrieve them."

"I fail to see why that is so amusing, but I am sorry, Adam. I came, Miss Sutherland, to check on the daily totals of pupils for last week."

"Yes sir, I have those figures right here, but Mr. Marshall, the class will need to use the privy at noon. Could you please drive and get Clarence to come with his fishing pole?" Mr. Marshall agreed, it was done, the glasses recovered and cleaned, and Adam was able to go home unafraid.

Julia wanted to ask Mr. Marshall about the results from the testing of Wissie and talk with him about the bruises on her arms, but he seemed to be in a hurry and she did not want to talk in front of the other children.

"Miss Sutherland," he said, "I have a meeting over in Kellston and I must hurry. The wind is picking up so I will drive Wissie home. Thank you for the attendance records."

Wissie left with him and Julia noticed that her doll was tucked under her arm and she was rubbing her wrist.

On Wednesday following the noon recess, Julia was reading <u>Paul Revere's Ride</u> to the class. The younger ones rested their heads on their desks during this time. She had reached the part that reads,

"One, if by land, and two, if by sea;
And I on the opposite shore will be,"

when the door opened, Little Budd entered, removed his hat and nodded to Julia. He walked over to Ben Hill, whispered in his ear and the two left the room. She knew that something very serious must have happened, and it was hard to finish the rest of the day.

When she reached home that afternoon Clarence told her that a 2 by 4 "flew off a c-chipping saw and ripped into Mr. Madden's left thigh and s-s-stuck out his back. L-Lil' Budd took 'im to the hospital in Macon and the doctors said he'd live but he was in b-bad pain." Julia knew that in all likelihood Ben Hill would not get back to school for many weeks. She was disappointed for him because he was trying to learn and he particularly enjoyed Fridays.

Fridays were usually Recitation Day, when the children had an opportunity to tell a short story or recite a poem before the class. She felt that this gave them a chance to practice memorizing and perhaps, to develop poise in public speaking.

On a Recitation Day in early March Ben Hill had surprised her by asking if he could recite a poem that he had written. "Yes, of course you may," she had said. His words surprised her even more. He had walked to the front, shifted his weight from one foot to the other and then back again, and without notes he spoke.

> "Naked branches traced against a deep blue sky,
> Dried yellow grass struggling to survive,
> Crumpled brown leaves swirling underfoot,
>
> Pyracantha berries red,
>
> Muscadine arbors dry and dead--
>
> Do you remember?
> That was November."

After a moment of silence, Julia had said, "Ben Hill, that was lovely. I would like to have a copy of it." A slow blush began at his collar and worked its way north to his eyebrows.

One of the Dunn twins had said, "Well it don't make no sense to me." Julia had given him a stern look as Ben Hill returned to his seat.

This week she had moved Recitation Day to Thursday because of the county-wide picnic scheduled for Friday.

Azalee Settle wanted to speak first. She came to the front of the room, cleared her throat several times, and said rapidly,

> "All the pretty things put by
> Wait upon the children's eye,
> Sheep and shepherds, trees and crooks,
> In the picture story-books.
>
> by
> Robert Louis Stevenson"

"That's nice. Thank you, Azalee," Julia said. "Who wants to be next?"

Donny's hand was already in the air. He came forward and said,

> "Proverbs 10. 'A wise son makes a glad father,
> but a foolish son is a sorrow to his mother'."

As he returned to his desk, Julia said. "Well done, Donny." She knew Clarence would be pleased with his selection.

Julia always took her chair to the back of the room while the children were reciting. It seemed to encourage them to look up and to speak louder.

Tabitha was now waving her hand. She lumbered forward, stood before the class near the stove, and announced, "I shall recite <u>The Village Blacksmith</u> by Henry Wadsworth Longfellow." She took a deep breath and using expression and broad gestures with both arms, she began.

"Under a sp-rea-ding chest-nut-tree
The village smithy stands;"

She stamped her foot.

"The smith, a mighty man is he."

Tabitha flexed her arms to demonstrate.

"his brawny arms..."

She had studied very hard and did not miss a word until she reached the line that reads,

"You can hear him swing his heavy sledge---"

To demonstrate this, Tabitha swung her heavy sledge-arm right into the flue beside her. It separated, crashed to the floor spewing soot and dirt all over Julia's desk and the floor, and turning Tabitha into a very large, dusty tar-baby.

It had been a long and eventful week and it was not over yet.

Chapter 22--A Problem

Mr. Marshall was scheduled to speak at the county-wide picnic about his goals for the three schools. Julia had anticipated going on Friday. It was not to be.

Classes were dismissed at eleven to allow plenty of time, but Lou Etta approached her as the others were leaving and asked, "Mis' Sutherlan', kin I talk to you?"

"Of course, Lou Etta, what is it?"

Lou Etta began to cry. "I don' know what to do---they counted on me to finish school---I can't tell them. I'm even scar't to tell Ben Hill. Mis' Sutherlan', layin' on the railroad track jes 'fore train time is all I can think of to do."

"Hush now Lou Etta, no. Don't talk like that." Julia dared to ask, "Lou Etta, what have you done?"

"Mis' Sutherlan'," Lou Etta sobbed, "I think I'm goin' to have a baby."

"Oh, Lou Etta, are you sure? I'm so s---" Julia stopped herself from saying how sorry and disappointed she was. "Are you sure?"

Lou Etta nodded, "Nobody knows but you. Ben Hill's havin' to work almos' all the time at the saw mill since his Pa got hurt."

She sniffed and wiped her eyes, "He leaves me notes in that fence post by the ol' Merrin place. That's where we used to meet, that ol' abandoned house. I do luv'im, Mis' Sutherlan'. I don' know what to do." The tears flowed again.

"Well, I don't know either, Lou Etta, but I do know that there will be NO more thoughts of the railroad track. You have a responsibility now for another life. I think you first should tell Ben Hill, then if you want me to, I will go with you to talk to your parents. Of course you will have to quit school, but perhaps you and I can have private lessons after I have finished with my school day and you could complete your work that way."

Lou Etta brightened. "Oh, Mis' Sutherlan', you reckon I could?"

"First I think we need to see what Ben Hill says, then we'll talk again."

Julia went immediately to talk with Dr. Weismann. The day was too cool for him to be sitting on the porch but, he answered her knock at the door.

"Dr. Weismann, I need your advice. I cannot tell you the name, but one of my pupils is expecting a baby. She is fifteen. She is so distraught she has even contemplated suicide. How can I help her? I am desperate."

Dr. Weismann sighed. "These things are a little like war---it's much easier to start such ventures than to stop them. I know of a place in North Carolina and another near New Orleans where she could go "visit an aunt" and then the baby would be available for adoption. But these homes are run by Catholic nuns, and some of the families around here would not like that. It is also a long separation from home. The other option would be a wedding. Is that possible?"

"At this point, I am not sure," Julia replied. "I could tell her parents about the homes. Thank you. That's helpful."

On Sunday afternoon Julia arranged a conference at the Mobley home. In attendance were Lou Etta and Ben Hill, his mother, Mr. and Mrs. Mobley, and Julia. Mr. Madden did not feel like getting out, but he knew about the baby.

Julia could feel the tension in the room. Mrs. Mobley and Mrs. Madden were obviously nervous, but were trying to remain calm and civil. Mr. Mobley, knuckles white from gripping the arms of his chair, looked back and forth from his daughter to Ben Hill. Julia could see on his face a mixture of emotions---fury, frustration, disbelief, and above all, overwhelming disappointment.

Quickly Julia said, "I spoke with Dr. Weismann and he told me of the possibility of Lou Etta going to a Catholic home where nuns would care for her and place the baby up for adoption."

"No." Mrs. Mobley said adamantly. "I don't want that for Lou Etta. There might be other places, but we cain't afford it."

Ben Hill had been looking at the floor as though he would like to vanish. He glanced up at Lou Etta. Their eyes met. He straightened and Julia thought he suddenly seemed to mature five years in less than a minute.

Looking at his mother and at the Mobleys he said, "I don't want Lou Etta to be away from Chalk Creek for eight months. Since Pa's accident I need to quit school anyhow and take over the sawmill. If Mr. and Mrs. Mobley don' mind, I'd like for me and Lou Etta to get married."

Lou Etta looked at Ben Hill. Pride and love mingled in her eyes and the smile that crossed her lips was like a ray of sunshine in the room.

Disappointment was still evident on Mr. Mobley's face, but he nodded slowly, still grim-faced. A wedding date for April 21th was set, one week from today.

Julia was grateful they had been able to resolve the situation without shouting or bloodshed.

Walking home the thought occurred to Julia, "Now Miss Carrie has a recipient for her new quilt."

With the decision made and a wedding date set, Julia could tell Rose.

Rose's reaction was, "Well, it ain't gonna hairlip the nation! In a few years nobody will remember. I'm living proof of that.

I'm proud that Benton Mobley could control hisself. I've seen him s'mad he wuz like hell stewed to a pint."

On Sunday afternoon, April 21th, with only the two sets of parents, Ben Hill's grandmother and the young teacher present, the Methodist Circuit preacher came to the Mobley home and performed the ceremony. Lou Etta looked lovely wearing Julia's lace-covered satin party dress with the pink bow.

Chapter 23--The Baptisms

It had been an uneven spring, one day cold and windy and the next day warm and sunny. After two weeks of heavy rains, the Ocmulgee was very muddy, and all the creeks were swollen several feet beyond their banks. Nevertheless, since the revival last month, there were four young people and old Mr. Struthers waiting to be baptized. In the woods redbuds were showing their distinctive reddish-lavender color, and Rev. Lucas had decided it was warm enough to hold a baptism service.

Shady Grove Baptist Church stood on a slight knoll in a clearing near the south bank of Reedy Creek. Under the old blackjack oaks that stood between the church and the murky waters of the creek, women for four generations had spread dinners on weathered planks, some nailed to trees and some supported by sawhorses. These were never moved. Homecoming Sunday, usually occurring in the fall, drew the largest crowd, but funerals and baptisms were also well attended and were festal occasions.

Baptisms were conducted to the side of the church where the creek widened and curved to the right. Here the bank sloped gently and the slow-moving water was calm and only waist-deep. About five hundred yards downstream, at the confluence of Chalk Creek and Reedy Creek, the channel narrowed, and the water churned and foamed around large boulders.

At this point the bank was steep and had been repeatedly washed back by the rapidly swirling flow. Several large willow trees tenaciously clung by a few roots to the high ground. Exposed, naked roots hung dangling toward the water, as though reaching for dirt to grasp. Reeds and tangled vines meshed thick along many places in the creek. Several miles downstream these waters emptied into the Ocmulgee River and thence, via the Altamaha, into the Atlantic.

On the upper side of the clapboard church, the Baptist dead of Chalk Creek, Georgia lay; some in neatly and lovingly tended plots, others under years of weed-covered sod. Two lone cedar trees standing like sentries at the top of the hill guarded the graves.

While Rose and the ladies of this year's Food Committee put out the dishes of fried chicken, beans, pies and cakes, Julia walked among the plots curious about the names and dates. She stopped at one family site and noted that Anna Scroggins, age 59, was buried there. On her headstone were carved the words:

Anna P. Scroggins
Born August 4, 1834
Married November 10, 1852
Died June 12, 1893

The striking thing was that next to her grave were nine smaller ones: four infants with headstones that had no names, only such information as: 1 month 20 days; 3 months 10 days; 2 months 4 days; and 6 months old. Next to these was one child of four years, another of six years, and three who died in 1866 of the Bloody Flux, their ages being five, eight and ten.

Julia could find no grave for a Mr. Scroggins. She wondered if he had died in the war and there had been no money to send his body home. This, Julia thought, was too much pain for any human to have to bear. Julia wondered if Anna Scroggins was pretty. Did she ever know a happy day, what were her expectations, her hopes as a young girl?

Someday, Rose would be in this place, and Clarence. What dreams and hopes did Rose have for her life? And when Julia's own name was carved in stone, what would it say? Would she have accomplished anything of value?

Walking on among the graves, Julia found that many other poignant family stories were evident in that small cemetery, but none so compelling to her as that of Anna Scroggins.

Immediately behind the church, a narrow path led to the unpainted privy. The entire area was fringed with small pines, a few red oaks and winged elms. In the moist places nearer the creek, box elder, black tupelo and bay crowded together and struggled for light. Thickets of plum and hackberry made walking difficult.

After the final hymn was sung, the small congregation filed outside and gathered along the banks of Reedy Creek. As she joined the group, out of the corner of her eye Julia saw Rev. Lucas' son and two other boys slip away from the group and run off into the woods toward the steep banks. They would be back by the time the meal was served, she thought. A few of the younger children were running and playing among the graves in the cemetery.

The three girl candidates for baptism were dressed in white. Mr. Struthers and young Peter Crawford were wearing white shirts and dark pants. The watching crowd of faithful worshipers were all in their Sunday best. A gentle breeze ruffled the large silk flowers on Mrs. Simons' Merry Widow hat, the one Rose said she had worn every year since her niece married in 1902.

The girls were baptized first, then Peter. Now it was Mr. Struthers' turn. Rev. Lucas guided him from the bank into the creek. Lowering the man under the water, he repeated the familiar words, "Upon your profession of faith in Jesus Christ, and in obedience to His command, I baptize you, my brother, in the name of the Father, the Son and the Holy Spirit. Buried unto death with Christ, raised to walk in newness of......"

The last words were never heard. From somewhere in the woods screams of terror drowned out all other sounds.

"Pa!" and again the call, "Pa, Mr. Braswell. Somebody, help!"

The nearest thickets parted and one of the boys ran into the open, "Help, Somebody, y'all help."

In the distance, from the steep bank of Reedy Creek, Julia heard someone shout, "It's a woman."

In their Sunday shoes and clothes, it was difficult for the men to move quickly through the swampy woods. Mr. Mobley, whose fire tower climbing seemed to keep him agile, was the first to reach the spot. When he returned visibly shaken, he explained. "When I got there Tommy Lucas and Melvin Wilcox were standing on the steep bank, white as sheets and pointing down into the swirlin' waters. I looked down and looking back up at us was a human face, badly bloated and rotted, with long brown hair tangled in the vines and roots that was holdin' it there."

Julia felt as stunned and shocked as everyone else. Two days later a small notice appeared on the back of page 3 of the Macon Telegraph. The headline read:

Body Found in Reedy Creek

The body of Miss Katherine Potter of Pittsburgh, Pennsylvania, former teacher in Chalk Creek, was discovered Sunday, May 5th. She had been missing since October. According to Chief Deputy Thomas Stanley of Riley County, it is suspected that she died of accidental drowning. She had no known survivors.

After church on his next Sunday at Shady Grove, Reverend Lucas held a memorial service for Miss Potter on the bank of Reedy Creek. It seemed an appropriate place. Her remains were buried on the hill near the cedar trees. With no family to notify, and even the boyfriend, Robert's last name unknown, there seemed nothing else to do.

On their way home from the service, carrying their empty dishes, Rose observed, "It do seem to me that women spend a lot of their lifes preparin' for babies an funerals."

Although a few voiced the opinion that Miss Potter had been so unhappy "down here" that she just might have committed suicide, most people in Chalk Creek accepted the deputy's findings of accidental death.

Rose was one of them. Her only comment was, "Well, it's good to git shet of what we didn' know."

Although she could not explain her reasoning, Julia was not entirely convinced that her predecessor's death was accidental. The body was so badly decomposed that any cuts or bruises did not show. Julia kept asking herself, "Why would Katherine Potter, an intelligent person, have been walking along the slippery, treacherous banks of that part of Reedy Creek?" There seemed to be no satisfactory answers.

Katherine Potter's uncompleted letter ending in the words, 'something evil---' kept recurring in Julia's mind. Also repeating over and over in her head were the words of Durrell Cochrane, ax in hand, saying, 'no g-damn teacher's gonna tell me what to do.'

Chapter 24--New Letters

Julia had not seen Bitty Budd since that evening they walked together to the school. She was surprised when he appeared in time for supper on the Friday after the baptisms. He brought her another box from home and two letters.

"I seen you got anutha' letter from France and I thought you'd want it right away." His voice was kind. Neither of them spoke of their previous conversation. If he were thinking about it, Julia could not tell.

"That was very considerate of you, Bitty Budd. Thank you."

After supper and Bitty Budd had gone, she opened the box and was delighted to find four Ballard Obelisk flour sacks and a lovely blue chambray dress with a white lace collar and white buttons. It looked as though it would be exactly Wissie's size. A letter from Papa was inside.

April 28, 1918

Dear Julia,

We hope you are well. Spring planting is under way and of course I have been busy. You know, like Noah, we Sutherlands are tillers of the soil. From the enclosed dress you can tell that your Mother has been busy also. Judson is doing well. No letter from George.

The only news from Conway is that the Gypsies, like the robins, returned last week to the Gypsy Woods. They left on Saturday. On Monday word spread around town that the oldest Fawcett girl (family down by the river whose son was killed in France) was missing. She is fourteen and was not at school and has not been seen. Sheriff Scott wanted to go after the Gypsies. He suspects that they took her.

The strange thing is that Mr. and Mrs. Fawcett did not want to pursue them. Mrs. Fawcett was reported to have said that, 'Well, she's bout grown, she'll be gone soon anyhow.' I suppose it will remain a mystery.

Has your Miss Potter ever written to Mrs. Wimbush? You are missed by all of us.

Your loving father,
W.A. Sutherland

Julia thought she would write them about Miss Potter, but she would say no more than the newspaper had reported. She did not want them to worry about her.

The letter from Stephen was dated March 1918.

Dear Julia,

There is little to write about and little to cheer the Allies. As you probably know, the Bolsheviks have signed a peace treaty with the Germans; Italy is in retreat; France and Britain are weak- ened by mutiny among the ranks and slaugh- ter in battles. The western front has experienced what some are calling the greatest artillery duel in world history. Rumor has it that General Foch will be placed in command of all allied troops. Perhaps this will help. As we go through small French villages and see the destruction everywhere, I find myself being so thankful that this is not happening on American soil and to any place where you are. I feel very sorry for these poor women. We set up our latrines and showers in a village, usually near the town square, and as we shower the women wait beside the draining water searching and grabbing for bits of soap that may fall into the water.

We move again early tomorrow.

Thinking of you,

Stephen

Once again Julia felt tears streaming from her eyes. She didn't understand what she was feeling, but she knew that she had been praying daily that he and George would come home safely.

She remembered Stephen's wonderful soft brown hair, strong-looking shoulders, sincere, penetrating blue eyes and happy quick smile, which he seemed to use often. Dancing with him was thrilling. Drying her eyes, she determined, "I will not let my heart and emotions rule my head!"

The other letter was from Amelia Sanders.

Dear Julia,

I was glad to hear from you and quite surprised to find that you are teaching in Chalk Creek. Where is it? I am wondering if you will go back to school and finish next year. My teaching situation here in Macon is quite nice. I have a third grade and I am living in a lovely home with a nice family.

You asked me about the Institute for Mental Retardation. Julia, I have checked with my principal and with the Bibb County Superintendent and they found that there is no such place in Macon. In fact, there is no testing being done here at this time. I hope this is of help to you.

Write again sometime.

Your friend,
Amelia

What did this mean? Julia thought. Why didn't Mr. Marshall tell me that no testing was being done? I don't understand. She wrote in her journal:

May 10, 1918

I am praying that the Father of lights will give me insight and wisdom to under-stand and handle this very perplexing, mysterious situation. What really happened to Katherine Potter? Had she discovered the 'evil' in Chalk Creek? Is anything really wrong?

Chapter 25--
Donny's Accident

On Saturday morning while Julia was in her bedroom re-reading her letters, Rose was working in the kitchen and talking to herself as she often did. Julia heard her exclaim, "Whew, it sure is hot for the middle of May, and I don't have on enuf clothes to flag a train." Julia smiled.

In a few minutes Rose said loudly, "Sari, do you call what you did in here sweepin' the kitchen?"

"Yes'm, I do."

"Well, you come back here and lick this calf over again. I reckon it looks like you gave it a lick and a promise. I kin see dirt in lots of places. Where's Donny?"

"He's down by the spring cuttin' some elderberry stems to make him a blowgun."

"Well you go tell 'im to come in here and wash his face 'fore he goes to the Lathem's. I don' like him playin' with those boys---they're a no-count fam'li. He'll probably get dirty while he's there, but he kin leave home clean."

"Yes'm. Kin I go and play with Eulalee?"

"After you finish sweepin'. If you don' stay more'n about an hour."

"Yes'm."

Rose busied herself in the kitchen cooking.

The children had been gone less than half an hour when Julia heard her exclaim, "Well, that wuz a short horse soon curried." This was followed by, "Oh my stars and body! What's wrong? Mis' Sutherlan', please come here."

Julia rushed to join her outside. Sari was trying manfully to support Donny as he hopped on one foot, his face distorted in pain.

Rose ran to help him up the steps, and asked, "What happened, Sari?"

"Ma, the boys wuz jes' startin' to play chasin'. Donny wuz 'it' an' he jumped off the porch an' landed on an' ol' iron rake kinda covered with leaves. One of them tines went clean thru his foot."

Gingerly Rose sat him at the kitchen table. "I tol' yawl I didn' want you playin' with them Lathems. It's no sin to be po'r, but it's bound to be a sin to be trashy. And that's what they are, trashy." She held Donny's foot and tenderly brushed away dirt.

"Mis' Sutherlan', would you look behind that curtain and on the bottom shelf see if you kin' find the carbolic acid..."

"No, Ma!" Donny cried.

"....and the bottle of turpentime and the Epsom salts."

Like a drill sergeant she barked another order, "Sari, go find me a clean chicken feather. Be better, Donny, if this would bleed."

Among at least a dozen bottles on the shelf, Julia saw a brown one with a label that read <u>20th Century Poultry Tonic</u>, a tall box labeled <u>Nash's C and L for Malaria Chill with Laxative</u>, <u>Praten Lice Killer Shampoo</u>, and <u>Benzo-Almond Cream</u>. Near the back of the shelf she found the Epson salts, the carbolic acid and finally the bottle of turpentine.

"Now Mis' Sutherlan', would ya' put jus enuf of that carbolic acid in a coffee cup to cover the bottom and then fill it up with water. That's right. Now, Donny, you hold on." She dipped and twirled the feather in the solution and ran it into the wound.

"Ow, Ma!" Donny yelled.

"If it don't sting, Donny, it ain't medicine, and it ain't doin' no good."

As if this were not painful enough, she then poured turpentine over his foot, "Sorry, trashy folks" she grumbled, "---never clean up their yard. Don' you ever let me hear of you playin' with them again. You hear?"

Donny moaned, "No'm,---uh, I mean yes'm."

As she worked on Donny's foot, Rose continued her diatribe. "Lillie Lathem use'ta come by here time after time ast'n me if I got any extra goat's milk or vegetables or anything."

"Ow! Ma," Donny winced.

"She al'us wanted turnip greens and corn. One time I 'member she come ridin' up here on a goat, her feet jes' bout draggin' the ground, with a cloud of mangy-lookin' cheerun trailin' behind her. She called out to me in a voice sweet as sorghum, 'Rose, you got any vegetables you could spar?'"

Again Rose poured turpentine over Donny's foot.

"She made me s'mad I come out on the porch and said, 'Lillie Lathem I'm gonna do better than that. I'm gonna give you some seed corn and some peas and turnip seed you kin plant'."

Julia said, "That was smart of you, Rose."

"You know what she said to that, Mis' Sutherland? She said, 'Rose I wouldn' do it, fer it.' I like never to 'uv got over that! Shiftless. Won't even hep theyselves--leavin' turned up rakes to rust---I don' know whut they had a rake for in the firs' place. Never use it."

"Ma, it hurts," Donny moaned.

Sari reached out and patted his arm.

"Sari, go look under my bed and find one of them ol' sheets in that box and bring it here." Rose directed. "She don' tell the truth neither. If she had a cow's tail hangin' out her mouth, she'd sware she didn' eat it."

Julia smiled and held Donny's foot while Rose heated water and made a solution with Epson salts. She tore a sheet into long strips and soaked these in the hot solution. Wrapping Donny's foot with one of these, she said, "I'll change this bandage several times today and 'til this wound heals we'll boil these bandages every night and hang 'em here by the stove to dry. He shouldn' have no infection."

Donny tested his foot on the floor and was able to hobble around on his heel.

Julia said, "Donny, you'll be a hero at school. The girls will want to carry your books."

Donny grinned and shook his head.

As she returned to her room, Julia overheard Sari tell Rose, "Ma, as we wuz hobblin' home Mr. Marshall passed us goin' the other way. He didn' stop. I think I saw Wissie in the car. It was a girl with a blue dress on. Wissie's worn that new blue dress 'most everyday. He could see Donny's hurt. Wonder why he didn' stop?"

Julia remembered that it was yesterday she had overheard Wissie talking as she played with her doll and a short stick. She had said, "Put this in mouth, then we have candy". Wissie had offered Julia a piece of candy and said, "My special friend gave it to me. I give you some."

Julia had asked, "Who is your special friend, Wissie?"

"Can't tell. He's m'friend. It's secret. Can't tell."

Julia stood in her room thinking of these words and of what Sari had just said. Why indeed did Mr. Marshall not stop? She thought of Amelia Sanders' letter and of Wissie's drawing. What did it all mean? What was happening here?

She changed her shoes and told Rose she was going for a walk. For some reason she felt she must try to find that clearing.

Chapter 26--The Clearing

Julia was not sure that she could find the old logging road that led to Mine #1. Where the dirt road came to a dead end, a pine forest, cut over many years ago, was now growing back with a preponderance of hardwoods. Sunlight filtered through the branches. An occasional white dogwood, like lace curtains in a dark window, brightened the shadows. In some places sand was deep and made walking slower.

The path she found was narrow and hard to follow but seemed to be leading in the right direction. Two large crows suddenly cawed their way skyward, angry at the human intrusion into their territory. Julia hurried along. Young pines, their branches struggling upward for sunlight, scratched her face. Blackberry brambles caught at her skirt tearing her legs and stockings. She felt she was in a bad dream, running but not getting anywhere very fast.

Squirrels rustling among the leaves and racing across the tree tops startled her. Her throat was dry, her stomach in knots of dread and fear. A sense of foreboding, of panic seized her. She felt she must move quickly but quietly, but what was she expecting to find? Should she call out for Wissie?

Nothing along the trail gave any indication that anyone had used it recently. Except for occasional rabbit droppings and deer tracks, in the dim light she could see no footprints, no broken twigs, no signs of life anywhere. Should she go back and try to find another trail?

As if to deliberately slow her down, a huge dead pine lay across the path just ahead of her. Much too large to step over, the woods covered with briars and thickets on either side, there was nothing to do but to sit on it as high as possible and try to swing her legs over. As she slid down the other side, her skirt caught on a sharp edge of the rough bark and held fast. Turning to rip it loose, Julia heard an eerie cry.

Hot tears rushed to her eyes. Her palms were sweaty, cold.

Now running, she didn't know where or why, her way becoming more and more narrow with undergrowth and bushes covering the path, the sound came again suddenly from somewhere up ahead. It froze her. It was a moan, like that of an animal-in-pain, a wounded animal. Julia knew she must find it. Ignoring the pain in her side and shielding her eyes from the branches and twigs that brushed her face, she hurried faster.

Again came the muffled sound---closer now. Then quite suddenly, there was no more trail at all. The way ahead was completely blocked by brambles, vines and a deep ravine covered with honeysuckle and wisteria. It looked as though it would be possible to reach the clearing by going around on either side of the gully, but the cry had come from directly ahead.

Julia wanted to scream. Why had she not told someone where she was going?

The sickening, animal moan came again, this time much closer. Trying to climb down the gully looked impossible. Sliding down seemed to be a better plan. Holding on to the vines helped.

Climbing the other side, Julia tried to melt herself to the embankment inching up by using roots, vines and protruding rocks.

The moan came again.

Thick bushes covered the crest of the embankment. Julia was grateful that a recent rain and the accumulation of many years of fallen pine straw helped muffle her movements. Quietly now she reached the top.

Then unmistakably, she heard a man's voice, low, guttural almost whispering. Pushing herself up just enough to get her eyes at ground level and peeping through the dense undergrowth, she realized she had reached, by a back way, the clearing of Wissie's drawing with the rocks and main path directly across from her.

What she saw in front of her filled her with disgust and cold fear. She could not swallow and for an instant she thought she would be sick. In the level clearing close to the edge of the kaolin cliff, no more than fifteen feet away from her, Wissie lay on her back on a bed of a few leaves and a small amount of pine straw. Flower petals were scattered beside her and her lovely blond hair, matted by sweat on her forehead and neck, spilled onto the ground. Mr. Marshall's trousers hung by the suspenders on the low limb of a small sweetgum tree.

She watched without breathing as one would watch an advancing rattlesnake. Mr. Marshall's shirt was spread on a nearby bush. Wissie's blue dress, with his underwear on top, was dumped in a pile on the ground. He still had on his high top black shoes, his garters and long black socks. They seemed to accentuate the whiteness of his legs and bare buttocks. He was on his knees straddling her and leaning back on his feet. His left hand was on one of Wissie's breasts. His right hand was tightly squeezing her left wrist, forcing her hand over his body and down between his legs.

Julia felt her face and neck grow hot.

"Take it, take it, you need to know," he growled, "look at it! Watch it!"

Wissie's face was buried in the doll she clutched in her right hand.

Julia did not think. She knew there was no time to go for help. She must deal with this. From somewhere deep inside her, screams came repeatedly, "No. No! No," as she scrambled up the bank into the clearing.

Stunned, Mr. Marshall leapt to his feet and backed away from Wissie. For a moment he seemed dazed, confused, then quickly the lust and anger that had been in his voice became a seething hatred in his eyes. Like a cornered badger, he lunged toward Julia with his hands aimed at her throat, snarling, "You meddling bitch! This is none of your affair---she needs to learn!"

At this moment Julia knew exactly what had happened to Miss Katherine Potter. Her death was no accident. This was the "evil" she must have suspected and later discovered.

There was time only to react. Julia dodged his first lunge at her and made the opposite side of the clearing.

Mr. Marshall turned, his lips curled, his eyes narrowed, calculating. Wissie lay between them rolled into a ball, softly crying. The kaolin bluff was too close behind Julia. She tensed, uncertain which way to move. She must get away from the edge. And then all at once, with the ferocity of a charging bull, he jumped over Wissie and rushed toward her again.

She never knew exactly how the miracle happened. She didn't remember seeing the wisteria vine as she had crossed that ground just moments before, but somehow the heel of Gilbert Dudley Marshall's shoe found it. Caught on a vine no larger than a half inch in diameter, he stumbled, and tried to right himself, but the force of his momentum propelled him forward. He stumbled again, tripped, and as Julia watched in horror, he fell head long into kaolin cut #1.

There was no sound other than Wissie's whimpering. The reality of what had happened came slowly. One moment there had been abject terror, the next moment it was gone. Julia edged to the cliff and looked down.

Sixty feet below on the rocky floor a pale naked man lay on his back. Partially open blue eyes stared up at Julia. From the back of his head and from his nose and ears blood trickled and was forming crimson pools on the white rock. There was no movement, no sound.

Gathering Wissie in her arms Julia whispered, "Let's get you dressed, Wissie. Don't cry anymore, it's over now. Let's go home."

Chapter 27--The Widow

Like a brush fire fanned by high winds, the news about Mr.Marshall spread quickly in Chalk Creek. People were asking, "How could this have happened? Why didn't we know?"

Mrs. Madden said, "You know I never really liked him"

Mrs. Simmons said, "You can't trust a man with shifty eyes. I never trusted him."

Benton Mobley said, "Well, he's damn lucky he died quick, and Durrell Cochrane didn' git a holt a him! He'd a-probably chopped off his hands, then a foot, then his dingy and left the sorry soul to bleed to death."

The nine-year-old girl over in Kellston had now told her story. Julia decided that a rendezvous with this girl must have been the reason Mr. Marshall was late for her interview with the school board.

Speculation ran riot on what had happened to Miss Potter that fateful day last October when she disappeared from Chalk Creek. Had she confronted Gilbert Dudley Marshall with her suspicions of his misdeeds? Did he choke her to death and then dump her body in the creek, or did he lure her there and then force her under the water until she drowned? These questions would never be answered with certainty, and seemed to Julia to lead only to more questions.

Julia wanted to go to talk with Dr. Weismann, but felt that first she must go to see Mrs. Marshall.

Little Budd offered to take her and wait outside.

Julia and Mrs. Marshall sat in the small living room.

After the initial condolences, Julia asked gently, "What are you going to do, Mrs. Marshall?"

Anita Marshall looked up from her damp knotted handkerchief. Her hands kept twisting, turning and untwisting it as though her efforts might somehow unravel the tangle of her life. "I don't know," she said.

Tears were spilling out of her eyes. From some bottomless void she drew an exhaustive breath and held on to it for a moment. Through clenched teeth the torrent of her miserable life tumbled out.

"I haven't made a decision in so long. I don't.....I don't know how to make one. Every decision I've ever made was wrong. I don't know how to think anymore. There was no need for me to think. I was never right, so he did all the thinking. I was always wrong.....or he could do it better. I don't know how to think anymore."

Her voice trailed into silence. Her hunched little body rocked like a metronome, propelled by some inner source of energy.

"Perhaps it's too soon to think, Mrs. Marshall. You really need rest. Could you go to your parents for a few weeks?"

"Oh, no!" Startled, she straightened. "I would never do that! They must never know. They are old, they thought he was wonderful. They believe I married well. It gives them something to hold on to, to think of me so well-off, married to a college man. I could never tell them. I don't know what I am going to do.....I trusted him when he said this place would be different."

"Do you mean there have been others, Mrs. Marshall?" Julia asked.

"Oh yes. He was told to get out of Tennessee, and before that it happened in Arkansas. He promised me it would not happen again. When we first met, he told me he was attracted to me because I reminded him of a little girl. I guess I should have known. I never thought it would lead to murder."

A wisp of thin gray-brown hair had fallen over one eye. Breathing in deep gulps she whispered, "I'm so tired---so tired."

Lifting her head slowly her gaze turned inward, down through a maze of painful memories into the past. With only the ticking of the mantel clock to break the silence, she struggled for control, biting her lips. Haltingly she said, "Some problems can be battled, others can only be borne. And they get heavy. Very heavy."

Tentatively Julia put an arm around her shoulders and suddenly a torrent of tears broke the dam of tension. Mrs.

Marshall's frail body heaved and rocked with surprising force. "I had hoped, so hoped, this place, this time would be different," she sobbed.

Julia did not know what to say. She hated to leave her alone.

For a long time on the way home in the truck with Little Budd, Julia was so overcome by her emotions she could not speak. Finally she said, "Little Budd, an English essayist once wrote that 'None are completely wretched but those who are without hope'. As great a gift as hope is to us, can it sometimes be a prison?"

Nodding his head as though he understood, Little Budd said, "Probably so, Miss Julia, probably so."

Chapter 28--Final Weeks

The next day Julia went to see Dr. Weismann. They sat on his porch in the warm sunshine of a May afternoon.

"Dr. Weismann," Julia asked, "do you think Dudley Marshall was born the way he was?"

"I don't know Julia. He may have been born with a tendency to deviate. That word in itself is very close to the word devil, isn't it?"

Julia nodded, "In these last few weeks I have seen so much of meanness and evil in this little community. I wonder, has mankind made any progress in two thousand years? Will we ever learn to choose what is right?"

Dr. Weismann shook his head, "Well, this earth is certainly no Paradise. It's more like a battleground. Wars between nations, fights between men, and struggles within men. Each of us must choose sides. There are no spectators. Dudley Marshall must have struggled against his demons every day."

He was quiet for a few seconds, then continued. "You know, three hundred years ago down in Santo Domingo doctors did an autopsy, the first known postmortem in the

New World, on the bodies of Siamese twins. Do you know why?"

"No, why?"

"They wanted to learn whether the twins had two souls or one."

"You are teasing me!" Julia smiled.

"I'm serious. Someday we may understand about people like Dudley Marshall, but not now."

Julia said, "I do hope Wissie can somehow find happiness in her life."

"Yes. And I have been wondering about you. Only two more weeks of school and then what will you do?"

"I'm not sure," Julia said. "I dread facing my mother. I defied her by coming to Chalk Creek, but of course I shall go home for the summer. I know that I should finish college and get my degree, but I do not think I want to spend my life teaching. I have enjoyed these children, but I have nightmares that I may end up like Miss Behn, an old teacher at home. She is forty-two and still proudly shows people her hope chest filled with beautifully monogrammed sheets, pillowcases, dresser scarves, underwear and even handkerchiefs."

Dr. Weismann threw back his head and laughed. "Old at forty-two?"

Julia smiled, "Rose says that women will never get over waiting for the right man. I want more than that. One part of me can see the value in a marriage like my parents have, or Rose and Clarence, but another part of me doesn't want to be tied down, limited by a husband and children. I want to do something important! There are a few female doctors and even a woman in Congress now; someday soon women will be able to vote. Our world is changing. I think of the opportunities, the problems, and my desires, and I cry out like Bunyan's Christian, 'What shall I do?'"

Dr. Weismann rubbed the back of his neck, then looked steadily at her. "Julia, do you not think that what you are doing here is *Important*? Isn't influencing the minds and lives of children about the most important thing you could ever do?"

She returned his gaze, thoughtful, but did not answer.

"The results are not immediate of course, perhaps you will not even live to see them, but you must realize that you are planting seeds that may bear fruit in the future of Georgia, even the nation."

Julia watched his eyes, quizzically, was he teasing her? But he continued, "From these simple, hard-working folk you may be helping to form future statesmen, educators, ministers---the possibilities are endless."

She glanced down at the floor, then into his kind face as he said, "I believe the God we both know gave women a special virtue---a creative energy, a desire, if you will--- to create something new where there was nothing before. Teaching, having children and having an interest in music, art or writing is all part of that creative energy. Why not business or politics?

Women are certainly strong enough, though maybe not mean enough."

He leaned back in his rocker, stretched his legs, looked slowly up at the sky, then at Julia and thought- fully said, "I believe you, as I did, will do whatever you are determined to do. But at what cost?"

He took off his glasses, blew on them and cleaned them with his handkerchief as he spoke, "It was a wise philosopher who said, 'the deepest need in man is the need to overcome his separateness, to leave the prison of his aloneness.' I hope you will not deny your need for love and family just to succeed in another world. I would like to think of you as doing both. At the end of life wealth might be helpful, fame could be temporarily exciting, but loneliness is no way to spend your last days."

For several seconds, Julia looked into his eyes. She wanted to thank him, to let him know how much he had helped her. Words seemed inadequate.

She rose, "You have been a valuable friend, Dr. Weismann. I don't know yet what I will do, but I do know that I will never forget our talks."

He stood and took both her hands in his. "You have made a difference here," he said. "Give it time, my dear. Give it time."

Walking up the hill toward home Julia was thinking about Mama. She realized that she had never wondered, never even thought about whether or not Mama was happy with her lot.

Was being a wife and mother what she had wanted to do with her life? She could have stayed single. Did she consider doing that? How do we know when we are young what we are going to want later? There's no going back to do it all over again. Julia felt that Mama expected her to finish school and "make a good marriage". Papa hoped she would make a good life. Julia knew that she would face many decisions in the coming months. She somehow felt more confident now to make them.

Two days later a jubilant letter arrived from Papa. He wrote:

> *Dear Julia,*
>
> *This week your Mother and I received a telegram from the War Department informing us that George had been wounded and was being sent to England. We know nothing about the extent of his injuries except that his sense of humor was not destroyed. Yesterday we received a cablegram from England that consisted of three words:*
>
> *DEBARKED DELOUSED DELIGHTED*
> *Love,*
> *George*
>
> *I, too, am delighted that he is out of the fighting.*

Your Mother and several ladies of the Decoration Day Flower Committee have picked dozens of Lilies of the Valley from the bed under our bedroom window. They are placing them today on the graves of the Confederate dead buried in Old Hebron Cemetery. They seem to enjoy doing this every year.

Your devoted father,
W.A. Sutherland

The days felt to Julia as though they were flying past her. During the last weeks of the school year there seemed to be so much more to accomplish, and so little time left. Many of the children had made real progress although others like Reavis and Leavis, preferred to play and enjoy life. Perhaps Dr. Weismann was wrong. Perhaps she hadn't made much of a difference here after all.

Working with Lou Etta after school hours was a joy. It was becoming evident now that a baby was on the way. She was studying hard, eager to learn, and Julia felt sad to leave her.

She prepared an examination for Lou Etta and felt that if the young girl could pass it successfully she would be able to go on someday to a state Normal School.

The English section included questions of grammar such as:

1. Name the parts of speech.
2. Define verse, stanza and paragraph.

3. What are the principal parts of a verb?
   Give examples with: do, lie, lay and run.
4. What is punctuation?
   Give rules for marks of punctuation.
5. Write a composition of about 150 words showing that you understand these rules of grammar.

The arithmetic exam asked her:

1. Find the cost of 6,720 lbs. of coal at $6.00 a ton.
2. What is the cost of 40 boards 12" wide and 16' long at $20 per meter.
3. What is the cost of a square farm at $15 per acre, the distance around which is 640 rods?

For United States history the questions were:

1. Give an account of the discovery of America by Columbus.
2. Relate the causes and the results of the Revolutionary War.
3. Tell what you can of the history of Georgia.
4. Who were the following: Morse, Whitney, Fulton, Bell, Lincoln, R.E. Lee, Penn and Howe?
5. Name events connected with these dates:
   1607, 1620, 1800, 1861, 1865

And on the geography test Julia asked:

1. What is climate?
2. Of what use are rivers?
3. Of what use are oceans?
4. What are the principal trade centers of the United States?
5. Name the capitals of four of the major nations of Europe.
6. Describe the movements and the inclination of the earth.

It was going to be hard to say good-bye.

Her plans were to leave Chalk Creek on June 4<u>th</u>, exactly five months after she arrived.

Julia had ambivalent feelings about going home. She was excited of course, but she dreaded having to face Mama.

Bitty Budd came to the house on that last Friday night. He brought her a letter from France, a small package from home, and a handful of wild hyacinths.

"Mis' Julya, Little Budd said to tell ya' that we'll bring the truck in the morn'n to take you to the train."

"Thank you, Bitty Budd. I hope you know I will miss you."

Bitty Budd ducked his head, then looked up at her and said, "Me, too, Miss Julya."

Stephen's letter was dated May 1918---Somewhere near the Marne River.

Dear Julia,

 The possibility of losing Paris seems to be very real. Going toward the front we often meet French troops going the other way. Sometimes I wonder if our two armies are fighting in the same war. Of course they have been in this for a very long time. We are headed for a place called Belleau Wood near the French town of Chateau Thierry. Paris is only 50 miles to our rear.

 You will be ending your school year soon. I shall write to you in Conway.

Thinking of you affectionately,
Stephen

Dear God, Julia prayed, please watch over Stephen.

Opening the small box, Julia stared in disbelief. Inside was a letter in Mama's handwriting and her gold locket. It was a short letter but it said all she needed to hear.

Dear Julia,

 We are looking forward to your return and we shall be at the station to meet your train.

Yours,
Mama

P.S. I think you are old enough now to have my locket.

235

June 4<u>th</u> dawned clear and warm. Julia heard Rose calling, "Mis' Sutherlan' com' here an' look at this!" Julia was surprised that they had come for her so early in the morning. In the yard the Budds had driven the truck almost up to the steps. The seat was covered with a quilt and large ribbons, some tied in bows, some hanging straight, were fixed to every conceivable spot.

"It looks as though you are happy for me to be leaving, Big Budd."

"No'm, that ain't so," Little Budd replied. "We just wanted the truck to look nice for you."

Rose and Clarence, Donny and Sari climbed into the back with Julia's trunk and Bitty Budd, and they bounced their way to the train. As they rounded the curve and bumped down the hill, Julia noticed a wide grin on Big Budd's face. Little Budd too looked as though he knew a secret.

The dust settled, the trunk was removed and the door of Hawkins store opened wide. Julia thought she had never seen so many familiar faces in one place. The Mobleys were there, the Dunns, Rev. Lucas, the Simmons, Mrs. Welborn and Tabitha Ruth, the Hardys and the Newmans. Mrs. Madden was in the crowd and of course Dr. Weismann. Julia looked up and saw Mrs. Alston waving from her wheelchair on her front porch.

Over by the side of the barber shop Julia noticed a parked car. Ralph was standing beside it. Inside she could see the small, bird-like figure of Mrs. Northrup. Jimmy Hawkins backed out of the store wearing his apron and sweeping the porch. He turned, and shielding his gesture with his chest, he shyly waved to her. Before the train came there was time to shake every hand and give Mrs. Alston a hug.

Julia was surprised and thrilled. But more than that, she felt humbled by these loving people, and challenged, by their demonstration of affection and respect, to become the best person she could be.

Julia overheard Mr. Mobley saying to Bitty Budd, "You know that sign hanging there don't look so good. Let's you an' me git a new chain an' fix it up. It looks like we don't much care 'bout Chalk Creek, don't it?"

In the distance the train whistle blew. Julia looked at Bitty Budd and noticed a tear on his cheek. She reached up and gently brushed it away. The fingers of his left hand pressed the spot, his chin quivered slightly, then a timorous, but proud smile moved the match stick between his lips.

To her astonishment she saw two figures coming down the hill. She recognized Wissie and Mrs. Cochrane. There would not be time to go to them. Waving and blowing a kiss to Wissie, she said to Little Budd, "Please drive them home. They have come all this way."

"I will, Mis' Sutherlan'."

The hardest part of leaving was telling Rose good-bye.

"Rose," Julia said, "I'm going to miss our talks together. You have taught me so much."

Rose looked surprised. "Naw, Mis' Sutherlan', I ain't."

"Yes, Rose. From you I've learned a lot about being content, about self-reliance, and character--- and especially about Mama."

She couldn't say it out loud but Julia knew she would also miss the child-like, yet profound way Rose had of looking at people and at God.

"Rose, will you do what you can to help Wissie?"

"Yes'm, I will," Rose whispered. "These cheerun' needs schoolin', Mis' Sutherlan'. I hopes you come back."

Julia couldn't answer. She did not know what she would do. She only knew that she had come to this place to teach, but she was the one who had done the learning.

Julia held Rose's hand as long as there was time, then stepped aboard the train to Macon.

THE END

Turn you to the stronghold,
Ye prisoners of hope.

Zechariah IX:12